FURTHER OFF FROM HEAVEN

FURTHER OFF FROM HEAVEN

Marlene E. McFadden

CHIVERS LARGE PRINT
BATH

British Library Cataloguing in Publication Data available

This Large Print edition published by Chivers Press, Bath, 1996.

Published by arrangement with the author.

U.K. Hardcover ISBN 0 7451 3941 8

Photoset, printed and bound in Great Britain by
Redwood Books, Trowbridge, Wiltshire

FURTHER OFF FROM HEAVEN

CHAPTER ONE

She had been out all day and still had no desire to return home. It had been hot, too hot, and now the sun was setting behind the hills in a red-gold blaze. There was an eerie stillness in the air which seemed to reflect Cassidy's mood, as though the whole world was holding its breath. Throughout the day, she had not spoken to a living soul but that was how she had wanted it. She had kept well away from the village, walking only where she knew she was unlikely to meet anyone else.

She had eaten nothing all day but an apple, and a bar of chocolate which had been unpleasantly sticky and melted in her hand. She was by now ravenously hungry and had a raging thirst which she had tried to quench by drinking from a stream. Her mind dwelled on Mam's shepherd's pie and home-baked bread, warm from the oven, thick with oozing, yellow butter, but not until her stomach was rumbling ominously did she decide to call it a day.

She whistled for Murphy, who had wandered off somewhere on a mission of his own, and the big, grey dog came bounding towards her. Still only a pup, he was enormous; long, wafting tail, shaggy coat, soft, dark eyes. He wasn't a full Irish wolfhound but had enough of the breed in him to give him the wolfhound look and size. Mam complained daily over the amounts of food it took to satisfy him and at the way he was continually under her feet, but Cassidy knew her mother loved the dog as much as she did.

How could she go to England and leave Murphy behind? Of course, that was an excuse she hadn't thought of. Perhaps it was one her mother would listen to. All the others Cassidy could come up with had fallen on deaf ears. She didn't want to go. She felt no loyalty at all to the old man—she could not bring herself to think of him as Grandfather.

It amazed her that Mam wanted her to go, that Mam thought the letter, the invitation, was some sort of honour. 'After the way he treated you, Mam? And never a word all these years,' Cassidy had said angrily.

Then she had run out of the house, Murphy following her without being bidden, and she had kept on running till she had left the village far behind.

But now, it was time to go home. Once the sun had disappeared. darkness would fall rapidly. Cassidy wasn't afraid of the dark. What was there to be afraid of? But Mam would worry and it wasn't fair to let her. It wasn't Mam's fault. Cassidy should not have spoken to her as she had. She should not have shouted, but she simply could not understand why her mother was so pleased he wanted her to visit him.

2

There must be a reason, some ulterior motive. The old man was over eighty now. He would be cantankerous and awkward. Age, Cassidy was certain, would not have mellowed him. Over twenty years ago, he had driven Mam away. He had given her an ultimatum. Choose Patrick O'Connor or your father. You can't have both. Mam, young, in love with the laughing-eyed Irishman, had not found the choice difficult. That she had lived to regret her decision was to Cassidy's mind neither here nor there. Because of Matthew Hawthorn's attitude his daughter Mary had been driven away from the family home.

She had given up her birthright. She had come back to Ireland, her mother's country and married her penniless, bone-idle Irish lover. He had loved her; words of love had come easily to his lips, but Patrick O'Connor was a man of changing moods and when the mood was black on him, he drank. When he drank he was violent and poor Mary took the brunt of it all. He died of a brain haemorrhage after being involved in a pub brawl two months before Cassidy was born. She had never known her father, but from her earliest years she had listened to her mother's stories about him.

Sometimes, Mam's eyes would shine with remembered joy as she told of Patrick O'Connor's winning ways, ready charm and Irish gift of the blarney. It had not been difficult at those times to realise why Mary

3

Hawthorn had cut herself adrift from her father to marry such a man. At other times, there had been tears and heartache. Cassidy as a little girl and later growing up had listened to it all, not wanting to hear it, not wanting to picture her father as a wicked man, but knowing it was Mam's way of getting it all out of her system. There had been no-one else to tell it all to. Life had been hard; and the two of them had grown up close as two sisters.

Cassidy was twenty-one now and a wage earner. Not much, it was true, but enough to make a difference to their family budget and she liked her job at the post office-cum-general store in the village, working alongside the postmistress, widowed Mrs Mulligan.

Mam told her time and again how lucky she was to get a job so close to home. Lucky to get a job at all, for there were many a one who hadn't and many a one who had had to go far afield to seek employment.

So why in the name of all that was holy had Mam got so all-fired up by the letter from England? It was like a royal summons, or an invitation to the hunt ball. *Mr Matthew Hawthorn requests the pleasure of the company of Miss Cassidy O'Connor* ... Did Mam want her to go away? Did she want to be left on her own? They had never been parted.

'Sure, it won't be for ever and a day,' Mam had said. 'You're due some holiday, Cass, and I'll speak to Bridie Mulligan on your behalf.

4

She'll understand. He's your grandfather when all is said and done.'

Fine time for him to be remembering that! He hadn't bothered to remember it before. How had he known where to find them, she had wondered. She had said as much to Mam and Mary had skated airily round an answer, giving Cassidy the distinct impression she was keeping something back, such as having been in touch with her father in the past, letting him know her whereabouts.

Now, why would she want to do a thing like that? It was all beyond Cassidy. Her mother had suddenly become a creature of contradictions. An enigma. So much so, that Cassidy wasn't sure she could believe anything she had ever been told. Perhaps the whole story of Patrick O'Connor was a myth. How would she know?

She was almost home. Murphy had already deserted her, bounding towards the house in eager anticipation of his supper. It was a neat little house, more of a cottage really, beyond the village and rather isolated, but the rent was cheap and it suited their needs. It would have been nice to have a bigger garden, Murphy especially would have liked that, and the bathroom was more like a cupboard with facilities, but it was home. Cassidy had known no other, though she well knew Mam had lived in far worse conditions with her father before she was born. Hadn't she been told so more

5

than once?

Cassidy's feet had taken on a leaden quality. She pushed her hands deep into the pockets of her jeans. She prepared herself to apologise. It was the least she could do. The door stood wide open. The air was cooler outside now the sun was setting but inside would still be hot.

The smell of supper cooking drifted out to meet her. Heatwave or no heatwave, Mam would have made a substantial evening meal. Cassidy's desperate hunger sent her running the last few steps into the house.

Mam was in the kitchen, stirring something in a large pan. She turned at Cassidy's approach, smiling, her hair damp on her forehead. Mam was so pretty, dark curls, deep, Irish-blue eyes fringed with long, dark lashes. She would laugh when Cassidy told her she was pretty.

'Oh, away with you!' she would cry. 'I'm forty-four years old.' She had been born in England of an English father, but no-one would know it to look at her for she was the spitting image of her mother, Elizabeth Cassidy Hawthorn, Cassidy's grandmother, after whom she had been named, and whose picture stood on the sideboard.

Cassidy was a surname, of course, and Mam had told her how Father MacIlvenny had frowned on such a name being given in baptism to a baby girl, but Mam had insisted. Cassidy had never discovered why it had been so

6

important to her mother, but she was satisfied with her name. It was different.

Her own looks, to her great disappointment, were very English. Dark-brown hair, dark-brown eyes. She was pale-skinned even in summer. Her hair was thick and short, cut in a smooth bob and her face had no trace of Irish in it. At least not to her. Not like her mother who was a real Irish rose. Cassidy was more like an English rose, something she did not particularly want to be.

'You look hot, love,' Mary O'Connor said. 'I've made some lemon and barley water. It's in the fridge.'

'Thanks.' Cassidy went and got a glass and opened the fridge door. The kitchen was small and square with barely the room to swing a cat round in. Certainly when Murphy was in there, and wasn't he always where he could cause most hindrance, there was nowhere to set your feet down comfortably.

Cassidy drank gratefully of the ice-cold liquid, wiping her mouth on the back of her hand.

'Oh, that was good!' She sighed.

'Supper won't be long,' Mary said.

Just as though they had never argued. Just as though there had been no letter and Cassidy had not stormed out of the house. She busied herself preparing Murphy's dinner while he lay there, patient now his food was on the way, his gentle eyes never leaving Cassidy's face.

'I'm sorry, Mam,' Cassidy said, forking dog meat into the huge brown dish and mixing it liberally with biscuits and a handful of bone meal.

'For what, love? Sure, and it doesn't matter.' Cassidy's mother was English, born and bred, setting foot in Ireland for the first time at the age of twenty, but her brogue was broader than Cassidy's own, as though she needed to forget her origins and think of herself as true Irish. The more Cassidy thought about her mother's character and ways the more she failed to understand why the prospect of Cassidy's going to England should have stirred her so.

'I've been thinking all day about his letter and—'

Her mother turned from the stove to look at her. 'He's your grandfather, Cassidy. He has a title.'

'Am I supposed to love and respect him?' Despite herself, Cassidy felt her anger begin to flare and crackle again, like a drawing fire. 'Is that what you want me to do?'

'Cassidy,' Mary spoke calmly, the wooden spoon in her hand dripping gravy on to the floor. Murphy made short work of the spillages. 'Just because Dad and I had our differences doesn't mean you should never meet him. He wants to meet you. You're twenty-one now and—'

Cassidy broke in. 'You had to leave home because of him, Mam. You had to leave

8

England!'

'Which is something I've never for one minute regretted.'

'Nor I.'

'So? Do we have to go on hating and hurting? Does that make any sense, Cass? Oh, maybe I blame myself. Yes, that's certainly true. I made you hate your grandfather. I should never have done that. Telling you tales—'

'Were they lies, Mam? Is that what you're saying, now?'

Mary shook her head vigorously, turning back to the stove and her stirring.

'No, oh, goodness, no, Cass. I told you the truth about Dad and Patrick, your father and me, but, well, maybe perhaps I didn't tell you everything.'

Cassidy flopped on to a chair by the kitchen table already set for supper.

'Then tell me everything now.'

'No, I can't. It's too late to go raking it all up. I want Dad to do that. Sure, if he hadn't written I don't suppose it would ever have occurred to me, not in a thousand years, but he has written, Cassidy. He's an old man now. Maybe he doesn't have a lot of years left. He wants to meet you. He wants to make his peace with me, through you.'

'Why can't you come to England with me, Mam?' Cassidy asked. 'I don't suppose I'd mind so much then.'

9

'No, I couldn't. I couldn't go back there. I couldn't adjust, but you—you're young; you've got all your life before you.'

Cassidy laughed. 'You've not exactly got one foot in the grave yourself,' she said.

'Maybe not, but I'll not be after leaving Ireland again, that's for sure.'

Cassidy set her chin stubbornly. 'I've no wish to be leaving, either.'

With alarming speed, Mary was at the table, banging it with her fist so that both Cassidy and the cutlery jumped with alarm.

'When he dies you'll get everything. He's a very wealthy man, Cass. He has no-one. Oh, I think you have a cousin. There was some mention of a cousin, but apart from him— don't you see, my love, your grandfather wants to see you for a very good reason? So he can leave you what he's got. I left home without a penny to my name and never a penny has he ever given me. I'm not going to stand in the way of you getting what is your birthright, Cassidy.'

There was a silence whilst Cassidy digested her mother's words. Then she spoke slowly. 'Was he telling you this, Mam? Did he say in his letter he was going to leave me everything?'

Mary looked away. 'No, not in so many words.'

'Then it's just your wild imagination running away with you again. As no doubt it's done so many times in the past.'

Mary gripped her daughter's shoulders so hard that it hurt. 'It's no imagination, child. There was the mill. Dad and his brother owned it outright. Well, Uncle George's been dead these many years. Ay, and his son Frank along with him.' She laughed shortly. 'Matthew Hawthorn, it seems, has outlived the lot of them, but maybe not for much longer and when he goes there'll be plenty, you mark my words, for he was never a man to squander his money. I should know that if no-one else does. So maybe you do have to share with a cousin of some sort. So what? It's your future, girl. Your legacy. Your right, and, by the Sacred Heart of Jesus I mean to see you don't miss the opportunity.'

So now it was said and Mam's hopes clear as the morning dew. Money. That's what it all came down to. They had never had much. Cassidy could remember a time when they were positively poverty-stricken. Never any new shoes or a dress for the school Christmas party. Even her First Communion dress had been made over from somebody else's. Times had been hard. Sometimes Cassidy had dreamed of someone rich coming along who would fall in love with her mother and sweep her off her feet.

She had dreamed this as much for her mother's happiness as for the money and security a knight in shining armour would provide them with. And all the time when the

11

dream inevitably faded into nothing, there was this stranger in England, their own flesh and blood who had everything that they had not.

Well, it was too late, now. Who did he think he was, this Matthew Hawthorn, who had taken a young, innocent Irish girl across the sea, married her and then, according to Mam, made her life a misery? Elizabeth Cassidy Hawthorn had died at the age of twenty-seven having borne three children. Mam had said very little about her sister and brother, and even less about her mother whom she did not remember, but there had been photographs and Mary O'Connor's tales. What was truth and what was fiction? Did it matter any more? Cassidy felt she was to be used as a sacrificial lamb.

She tried to make light of it all. 'What do we want with money, Mam?' she cried. 'We have each other.'

'It isn't enough, Cassidy. Oh, I've prayed for something like this. I've lit so many candles you wouldn't believe. And every year, on your birthday, I've written, and—' Mary broke off. She straightened up and guilt spread in a dark flush across her face.

'You've written to him?' Cassidy prompted, ice forming round her heart. 'Go on, finish what you were going to say. Have you been after sending the old man *begging* letters, Mam? You have, haven't you? And there you were trying to make me believe his letter came out of the blue. Well, you've been wasting your time, for I'm not about to set foot in England. I don't want anything of his. And you may as well put that on your needles and knit it!'

She was prepared to argue long and hard because it was no use pretending other than an unholy row would get her her own way. She did not want to visit the old man. She would not visit him. She had to use everything in her power to force her mother round to her point of view. What Cassidy was not prepared for was the tears that suddenly flooded her mother's large blue eyes; the trembling lips, the hurt that was evident in her face.

'Oh, Cassidy,' Mary sobbed. 'Please, I'm begging you. Don't let me down. It means so much to me and I don't want you to live to regret a hasty decision. And I know you will. You think you hate your grandfather and that's my fault, I know it. I want to put that right. Give him a chance, give yourself a chance. He isn't a monster, though perhaps I made him seem one to you. He's an old man, Cass, so give him the opportunity to make amends, to forgive and to be forgiven. Will you do that for me? Oh, darling, I'll never ask another thing of you for as long as I live.'

As the bubbling pan on the stove bubbled right over the top, hissing on to the gas ring and Mary flew with a curse to turn off the gas, Cassidy felt her freedom of choice, her willpower, dwindle alarmingly. She was going to lose. She could stand firm against most things, but tears went right to the heart of her. Perhaps Mam knew this. Was she using tears as a weapon? If Cassidy dug in her heels, could the battle go on and on, with neither of them yielding or giving quarter? But what sort of victory would that produce for either of them? Cassidy knew in that moment she could not do it. She went to Mary and put her arms around her mother, resting her head against Mary's shoulder.

'Oh, Mam, you're a terrible woman so you are!' She sighed.

It was enough. Mary O'Connor forgot the overboiled stew and gathered her daughter to her, her heart swelling with happiness.

CHAPTER TWO

It was a rough crossing, at least to Cassidy it was. Despite the mild weather, she felt sick for most of the time, huddling in a corner, shivering with cold and misery, wishing she could die. Once she left the ferry, however, she felt better immediately and was so hungry that she went into the station buffet, before continuing the next stage of her journey, and ate two ham and tomato sandwiches and three slices of fruit cake. The cost, including two cups of tea, nearly made her faint from shock.

It was the middle of the afternoon and Cassidy's next job was to find a phone and make a call to the post office to leave a message for Mam. Mrs Mulligan had agreed to pay for the call provided Cassidy was brief. Just a quick call so Mam would know she had arrived safely in England. That over with, she had to sit and wait for her train. She knew she had another long journey and that she would have to change trains. Finally, she was to take a taxi from the station in Liddensfield that would take her to her grandfather's home.

It was impossible for her to be met. Matthew Hawthorn rarely left his house and apparently his elderly housekeeper had no wish to put herself out. Cassidy was not looking forward to her meeting either with the old man or his housekeeper. Both would surely be formidable beings who would terrify her.

It was the fear of the unknown that was the worst, and being alone, of course. Cassidy was far from being a seasoned traveller. She had made occasional trips into the city, but she was never happy in crowded, busy streets. Her mother had tried to describe Liddensfield as best she could—allowing for the inevitable fact of changes over the years, but without actually seeing the town Cassidy's imagination served her up with images of looming buildings, banks, building societies, shops, people; unfriendly people, rushing here and there, with never a word of greeting. Hard, cold

15

pavements beneath her feet; dirt and grime, for Liddensfield was a large, industrial town.

Mary O'Connor had hastened to assure her daughter that the town of her birth also possessed a fine library and art gallery, many beautiful parks and that the town was surrounded by hills and some wild and wonderful country, being on the edge of the Yorkshire Dales and not all that far from the moors, Haworth and Brontë land.

Cassidy knew full well this last gem had been imparted as a sort of incentive. Mam knew that 'Wuthering Heights' was one of her favourite books, but when she asked eagerly, 'Oh, does Grandad live near Haworth? Will I be able to go there? Walk there?' Mary had looked apologetic.

'Well, no, Cass, not really,' she had admitted and Cassidy's spirits plummeted again. She might have known it. It was just a sop!

Grandfather Hawthorn did not live in the town itself and for this small mercy Cassidy was grateful. He still lived in the same house where Mary had been born and raised. The Hawthorn family home, situated on the edge of a rural village some four miles from Liddensfield. The word 'village' conjured up visions of home to Cassidy—green fields, stone cottages, peat fires in open hearths with smoke curling from chimneys, but Berrybridge, Cassidy had been told, was not like that.

Oh, there were fields and hills, but the houses

were built in terraces rather than sprinkled higgledy-piggledy here and there, for Berrybridge, in its heyday, had housed the workers at the Hawthorn woollen mill. Small, dark houses overshadowed by the mills, long since closed down, sold and now, so Mam said, divided into various units, rented out to different individual businesses.

On the last lap of Cassidy's long journey, the worst lap of all, she saw the Hawthorn mill and it was nothing like she had imagined it, nor was Berrybridge itself. The houses, and there were so many of them, seemed to be built one row on top of another, up into the wooded hills beyond the village. Opposite the mill was a church, the church where the Hawthorn babies had been christened. A Protestant church, but Mary Hawthorn, on becoming Mary O'Connor, had changed her faith and Cassidy wondered where the nearest Catholic church was. Today was Wednesday so she had four days to find out.

The taxi, on leaving the town centre, had travelled a main road route for what seemed rather more than four miles to a bone-weary and frightened Cassidy. It was hot and stifling and the driver was morose and unhelpful and drove like a maniac. He never got out of the driving seat and left Cassidy to haul her own luggage in and out of the taxi at both ends of the journey. She had given the address in a whisper, but the driver seemed to know where it was, taking the roads, the up-hills and down-hills, with ease and over confidence.

Eventually, they went over a hump-backed bridge where, far below, a trickle of water moved turgidly over the rocks and stones. A river, no doubt, when there had been rain, but now a pathetic imitation of one. Then there was the mill on her left, or what had been the mill and the old stone of its walls had been cleaned and the windows of the individual units shone. The church opposite was set in a badly-neglected churchyard, giving it an unused, forlorn appearance. Gravestones, green with age in places, stood sentinel over ancient, uncherished final resting places. The sight did not help to boost Cassidy's low morale.

One more twist and turn in a very twisty, turny narrow road and the taxi came to a jerky halt.

'Here you are, miss.' To Cassidy's amazement the taxi driver turned to smile at her—probably hoping the flash of his gold fillings would reap him a handsome tip. 'Berry House!'

'Thank you.' He still made no attempt to leave the driving seat and Cassidy picked up her suitcase from the floor, once again disgusted that no space in the boot had been afforded her. Did she have the courage she wondered to reflect her disgust by offering no tip at all?

'That'll be five pounds fifty,' the driver announced pleasantly. Ah yes, definitely ogling for a tip!

Cassidy opened her purse and paid him, plus tip, coward that she was. He left her standing on the roadside and roared away, back the way they had come, after executing a clumsy, noisy U-turn.

Cassidy looked up at the house. It was set well back from the road at the head of a gravel drive. No doubt the taxi driver had thought it wasn't necessary to take her right to the door. Blank windows stared down at her, each window framed in neat white curtains. There were lawns on either side of the drive, parched and brown now because of the summer drought. Mature bushes and trees stood regimentally along the boundary walls.

She walked up the drive, feeling more scared with every step. A brass knocker in the shape of a fox challenged her to beat it against the stout, wooden door. The brass shone, the sign of devoted and regular polishing. The windows shone, too. The housekeeper was evidently a house-proud woman.

The knocking on the door seemed to reverberate around Cassidy. Foolishly, her legs were shaking. Another minute and she would have turned tail and fled back down the drive and would not have stopped running till she got back to Ireland. But suddenly, she could hear footsteps, firm, plodding,

19

approaching the door, which opened to reveal a black-and-white tiled hallway where a short, plump woman of late middle-age was standing. The woman wore a neat navy-blue dress with a small, white collar. Her grey hair was soft-looking and slightly wavy. She wore large glasses with oddly incongruous blue-and-pink frames which, nevertheless, suited her round face. A pleasant face, not at all like the dour visage Cassidy had expected and dreaded.

'Why, Miss O'Connor, you're here at last.' The woman beamed, opening the door wider. 'Come in, lass, come in. I'm Mrs Dawson. Your grandad's housekeeper.' She held out her hand and Cassidy extended her own. Mrs Dawson's grip was firm, strong, reassuring.

Cassidy began to feel better. The hall smelled of furniture polish and, though rather gloomy, was in no way intimidating. A dark staircase curved upwards at the end of the long corridor, turning at a large window comprised of blue, green and red glass, which did not let in much daylight but was attractive, even church-like. A red, patterned carpet covered the stairs and dark, painted doors led off the hallway.

'My, you have come a long way!' Mrs Dawson went on cheerfully, relieving Cassidy of her suitcase and waving aside her protests. 'I expect you're famished. Well, I'll let you see your room first. Let you have a bit of a wash if you like.'

She started up the stairs; obediently Cassidy

followed, aware that so far she had not spoken a single word. Not that she had had the opportunity to do so.

'Then I'll get your bite to eat. Your grandad's fair waiting to see you, lass, but I said, "Well, you can wait. A few more minutes isn't going to make all that difference after all these years." I told him not to appear till I gave him the OK. Didn't want you to be put off, did we?'

Cassidy didn't know whether to be cheered or otherwise by Mrs Dawson's words. She was relieved that she hadn't had to meet the old man straight away. On the other hand, his housekeeper made him sound overbearing and unapproachable. Whatever he was like it seemed he took notice of Mrs Dawson, and if his own employee could give him orders he couldn't be so bad, could he?

The housekeeper led the way along a narrow passageway off the upstairs landing, opening a door with a flourish.

'Here we are, love. Hope you like it. We're not used to having a young woman around so you'll have to bear with us till you get used to us.'

The room was large and old-fashioned with heavy, dark furniture and a square of faded, green carpet laid over a polished floor, but everything was spotlessly clean and the same white curtains fluttered at the wide open windows.

21

Cassidy was quick to notice the house backed on to a wood and that her room had this peaceful view of trees in summer leaf. Perhaps it wouldn't be so bad here after all. There had been the river and the hump-backed bridge. Now the wood. She began to relax. Mrs Dawson was so friendly. Even her grandfather might not be the ogre of her imagination.

She spoke at last. 'It's lovely!' she said.

'Well, it'll do,' Mrs Dawson conceded, going and smoothing her hands over an already immaculate, rose-pink bedspread. 'You've plenty of drawer space and a good-sized wardrobe. The bathroom's at the end of the passage. Nothing fancy, mind you. This is an old house and between you and me could do with a bit of money spending on it, but there you are!' She paused for breath, beaming at Cassidy. 'Now, I can't go on calling you Miss O'Connor, can I, so what's your first name, love?'

Cassidy smiled in return. 'I'm afraid it's Cassidy,' she said.

'Cassidy?' Mrs Dawson repeated. 'A bit unusual, but pretty.'

'It was my grandmother's maiden name.'

'Oh, yes, I believe so. Course that was before my time though. I'm sixty-five, you know.'

Dutifully, Cassidy said, 'You don't look it.'

Mrs Dawson chuckled. 'Good, clean living and plenty of plain cooking, that's my recipe,' she confided.

Cassidy felt at ease enough to sit down on the edge of the bed. The mattress was high and firm. 'Have you been with my grandfather long, Mrs Dawson?' she asked.

'Fifteen years. Living in, of course. I came soon after my husband passed away. God rest his soul.'

Almost without thinking Cassidy crossed herself. Mrs Dawson tut-tutted gently.

'I shouldn't be doing that in front of your grandad. He doesn't hold with what he calls a lot of fuss and palaver. I'm chapel myself, of course, but your grandad's nowt in particular. Never sets foot in a church from one year's end to another.'

Cassidy felt a return of her misgivings. 'I—I would like to be able to go to Mass,' she whispered. 'Would you be knowing of a Catholic church around about?'

'Don't you worry, love.' Mrs Dawson's homely voice was strangely comforting. 'Come Sunday, I'll have told you how to get to St Joseph's. It's a fair distance and'll mean you going by bus, but you're a young, capable lass, I can see that. Is it just two weeks you're here for, Cassidy?'

'Just two,' she nodded, and it would no doubt seem like a month of Sundays.

'Well, I'm sure you'll have a nice time. I'll let you alone, now. Come down when you're ready. Your grandad's waiting to have his dinner with you.'

23

'Oh, is he?'

Her consternation must have been obvious because Mrs Dawson's loud chuckle rang out again.

'Nay, lass, he won't eat you! Don't look so worried. I'll let you into a little secret, shall I? He's been like a cat on a hot tin roof waiting for you to come. There's been no dealing with him, especially when he wasn't all that certain you would come. Well, here you are and a bonny sight and no mistake.'

The housekeeper went at last and after her footsteps had died away, the house seemed silent and empty. It seemed to be a large house, if the number of doors was anything to go by, built solidly, as old houses used to be, thick, sound-deadening walls.

Cassidy sat and looked around her. Well, she was here and she was starving but she doubted she would be able to eat a morsel. Not if she had to sit at the same table as the old man. What would he look like? Mam had no pictures of him, not even an old one. Would he be tall or short? Heavy-built or slender? Would he have a strong, dominant way with him? Cassidy comforted herself with the knowledge that Mrs Dawson had worked for him and lived in the same house as him for fifteen years and it had not apparently crushed her exuberance.

She got up and started to unpack her case. Then she remembered something. She had

24

tended to let slip her mind that the old man had driven Mam away from here. He had flatly refused even to meet young Patrick O'Connor and had forbidden him from the house. Mam left under a cloud, never to return, though perhaps as had lately seemed likely, she had kept in touch in some ways, the rift had never really been healed between them.

Cassidy O'Connor was as Irish as they came; a practising Roman Catholic who had holy pictures by the side of her bed (she had brought them with her) and a mother-of-pearl-backed Missal that she read every day. How could her grandfather ever accept her?

She should never have come and Mary Hawthorn O'Connor had a lot to answer for, so she had, for practically forcing her to do so.

* * *

The moment of dread could not be put off any longer. Cassidy was washed, changed and ready to go downstairs, but she still lingered in her bedroom. It had not helped to calm her fluttering nerves when she heard a deep, booming male voice coming up from below. Whose could it be, but her grandfather's? It was only momentary as though he was passing from one room to another, but it sounded so loud. How could she face him? What on earth would she find to talk about?

She stood looking out of the window at the

cool shadows of the wood. Oh, how she wished she was in that wood, walking among the sheltering trees. She liked woods, finding them havens of peace and solitude and this one looked inviting. Murphy would love it, hunting for rabbits, rooting in grassy hollows. It was the first thought she had spared for her dog since leaving home and caused her a sharp pang of homesickness. Would it be too much to hope that her grandfather kept a dog? She had certainly seen no sign of one.

Cassidy moved from the window and looked at herself in the dressing-table mirror. She had put on her favourite emerald green, cotton dress. It was sleeveless with a pointed, white collar and a row of tiny, white buttons down the front. It made her look absurdly young, but its colour had not been randomly selected. Emerald green for the Emerald Isle. She hoped the old man would grasp the implication of her dress.

She had brushed her hair vigorously and put on a little make-up, not a great deal, just enough to try to make her pale cheeks seem less pale. She was wearing tights though she always felt uncomfortable in them, but had felt for her first meeting with her grandfather she should be a little formal. Low-heeled shoes completed her outfit.

Her sombre, dark eyes looked out at her. She spoke crossly to her reflection. 'Go on, Cassidy O'Connor, face up to it. The problem's not

26

going to go away!'

She squared her slim shoulders and turned away from the mirror, walking resolutely to the door. On the landing, she hesitated briefly before walking, head erect, downstairs and into the lion's den.

She had gone only part of the way when the door to the right of the front door opened and out came a tall, thick-set man, erect and proud looking. He had a head of thick, white hair, a bristling moustache and sharp, keen eyes that soon latched on to hers so that she looked away blushing. He wore a white, starchy shirt, a brown, tweedy jacket and ill-matching, blue trousers, old-fashioned, though well cut, and he rested his right hand on a supportive walking-stick.

Cassidy knew he was past eighty years, but could hardly believe it. He looked ten years younger and when he finally spoke, his voice was firm and strong. In a few short seconds she experienced and empathised with her mother's inability to stand against this man or to win him round to her way of thinking.

'Well, come on, lass, let's have a look at you.' His accent was broad and flat, his manner brusque.

Cassidy prayed Mrs Dawson would materialise but she prayed in vain. She continued on her shaky way down the stairs till she stood in front of him.

'How do you do, Grandfather?' she said

27

politely, hoping her voice was not shaking too badly, but sure it was.

'I'm very well, thank you. And you?'

'Yes, thank you, Grandfather.' She could not look at him; she could only study the toes of her shoes and the highly-polished ones of his. Until he put a finger under her chin and lifted up her face and short of closing her eyes which she could not very well do, she had to look at him. His eyes were grey and they were twinkling brightly. He was smiling, a wicked, half-teasing smile.

'Afraid of me, lass? Nay, I hope not. I'm your grandad, and that's what I want you to call me. None of this "Grandfather" rubbish. So you're Cassidy, our Mary's lass? Well, you're not like her. Not a bit.'

'No, I know.' Cassidy felt wary. He was being friendly but why did she feel as though she was about to take a walk across very thin ice?

'Oh, do you? Like your dad, are you?'

'I never knew Dad, Grandfather ... er, Grandad,' Cassidy said, but she did know she didn't resemble the blue-eyed, curly-haired Irishman, either. She was herself. If he tried to find likenesses to other people in her he would look for ever.

'No, course you didn't.' His smile faded a little and his voice was quieter. 'Well, you're very welcome, lass, and not before time, and there's faults on both sides that's prevented us

28

meeting earlier. We only have two weeks to get to know one another, but I hope it'll be long enough. And I hope it'll be the first of many a holiday you'll spend here. Now, I expect you're that hungry you could eat a horse, but first off I want you to meet somebody else. Might as well get the introductions over all at once, eh?' He put his arm around her shoulders and propelled her into the room he had just vacated.

A sitting-room, with leather chairs and settee, not new either, but old and well worn, with comfortable-looking flowered cushions. There were tables here and there with vases of flowers; there was a gleaming piano, open, with music propped on it as though someone had recently played it. And in front of an old-fashioned, tiled, fireplace with a high, dark wood mantelshelf stood a tall, good-looking young man, smartly dressed, hair short and fair.

'This is your cousin, Leslie, Cassidy,' her grandfather announced. 'Leslie, meet Cassidy O'Connor.'

The young man came forward holding out his hand. Cassidy felt numb and responded automatically to the handshake. This was something for which she had been totally unprepared and she didn't like it one little bit.

CHAPTER THREE

Leslie Hawthorn was not, in fact, Cassidy's cousin, only her half-cousin, being the son of Mary O'Connor's cousin, Frank, and grandson of Matthew Hawthorn's brother, George.

'Hardly related to you at all,' he said with a dazzling smile on being introduced. A remark which only achieved significance much later.

Leslie was an orphan and lived alone in another village on the other side of Liddensfield. There were many such semi-rural communities on the boundaries of the large town. He described his house in great detail to Cassidy and she tried to nod and smile in all the right places but could not really visualise the random stone, split-level bungalow with integral garage. It sounded very modern and very expensive and Cassidy wondered how Leslie could afford such a house. He had, however, as he also explained, a very good job as an estate agent, a business he shared with one other partner, so that perhaps explained the house.

Leslie was twenty-four and had charming manners, which contrasted sharply with Matthew Hawthorn's bluntness, but by the time that first evening was over and Cassidy was preparing for her first night in Berry

House, she had begun to realise that her grandfather's bark was definitely worse than his bite and to believe she could eventually lose her awe of him and, indeed, come to like him, whereas Leslie quickly began to grate.

He seemed over-eager to please and impress her. He waited on her at the dinner table as though he had prepared the excellent roast-beef dinner himself, and was desperate for her approval. He rose when the meal was over and helped her out of her chair, leading the way into the sitting-room where Mrs Dawson had set the coffee tray. At one point Matthew barked, 'Leslie, for goodness' sake back off. Stop mothering the lass.'

Leslie, not in the least put out, continued to smile brightly and said, 'Now, Grandad, I'm only being polite and helpful. Isn't that what you've always taught me? To have good manners?'

'Good manners, perhaps, but give the lass breathing space.'

Leslie, Cassidy realised, tried to hide his Yorkshire accent but the result was a pseudo-posh voice which did not sound natural. Cassidy liked the way her grandfather spoke. He had no airs and graces, nor had she. And yet, he seemed genuinely fond of Leslie and it was apparent from their conversation that they met often.

Was Leslie to be around all the time she was there? She hoped not.

31

When they were settled drinking their coffee, Matthew made another blunt remark. 'Now, Cassidy, don't go running away with the idea that we eat like landed gentry every day of the week. Mrs Dawson generally makes a dinner at mid-day. Then it's high tea, if you want to be giving it its Sunday-best name. We're only having a big meal tonight in your honour.'

'You—you shouldn't have gone to all that trouble,' she stammered awkwardly.

'Of course he should,' Leslie cried. 'Personally, I prefer a light mid-day lunch and an evening dinner.'

'Ay, well you would,' Matthew said shortly and then, to Cassidy's surprise, he gave her a broad wink. His action pleased her.

Coffee finished, Cassidy stole a look at her watch. It was still only nine o'clock, but she was beginning to feel very sleepy. It had been a long day for her. She was afraid she might start to yawn any minute now, but did not have the courage to excuse herself. Not that she was contributing much to the conversation, only answering questions as they were put to her and in between sitting looking at her hands folded in her lap.

'How about going for a walk with me, Cassidy? It's a lovely evening,' Leslie said.

Her instinct was to cry, 'Oh, no, I couldn't, some other time maybe,' but Leslie had already leaped to his feet, holding out his hand to her and with a weak smile she allowed herself to be hoisted out of the deep, comfortable armchair where she could easily and blissfully have nodded off.

'Best put something else on your feet, lass,' her grandfather advised.

A sensible suggestion and Cassidy hurried up to her room to find a pair of flat sandals. She stayed there as long as she could. Perhaps if she waited long enough Leslie would get tired of waiting and leave. But no such luck; after only a few moments he was calling jovially up the stairs, asking if she had got lost. Reluctantly she drew her gaze away from the supremely comfortable-looking bed and went back down. Once more, Matthew Hawthorn was standing in the sitting-room doorway and Leslie was opening the front door where Cassidy could see the late evening sun was setting and smell the scent of flowers drifting in.

'I'll say good-night, lass,' her grandfather said. 'Old codgers like me need their beauty sleep. I'll see you in the morning. When you come back, just drop the latch. Mrs Dawson'll have retired by then, no doubt.'

How long did he expect her to be gone?

'Good-night, Grandad,' she murmured, hoping he wouldn't expect her to kiss him.

'Good-night, Grandad,' Leslie echoed.

'And don't make an unholy din, lad, starting up that jalopy of yours,' Matthew advised.

Leslie looked hurt. 'My car doesn't make a din. She purrs. As she should, she cost enough.'

Cassidy shot him a glance. He was deadly serious. Couldn't he take a joke?

She followed him outside, feeling even more disinclined to accompany him on his walk. He proudly pointed out the sleek-blue car parked at the head of the drive. Obviously expecting her to be impressed.

'I'll just leave my jacket,' Leslie said, removing the same. 'It's still warm, isn't it?'

It certainly was, and it seemed to herald a long, sleepless night. Oh, dear, perhaps the walk wasn't such a bad idea after all, to put her in the mood for sleep, but she would have much preferred to go for a walk alone.

Leslie rolled up the sleeves of his white shirt and unfastened his maroon tie. He gave her another of his dazzling smiles.

'Where to? Anywhere, I suppose, as it's all new to you. Do you fancy the wood?'

Cassidy declined, wanting to save that bit of exploring for when she was alone.

'Let's just look around the village,' she suggested.

'Sure,' Leslie said, putting his hands in his trouser pockets.

'Why do you call him "Grandad"?' Cassidy asked. 'He isn't your grandfather, is he?'

'Technically, no, but my own died when I was a baby and he was my great uncle's brother. Great Uncle Matthew! What a mouthful! I can't very well go around calling him that, can I?'

Cassidy didn't see why not.

'No, not really,' she lied.

They walked along the narrow road where the taxi had brought her earlier in the day. It seemed light years away. Already she was beginning to feel she knew the place. They passed a couple of small shops, one a post office-cum-general store like the one at home, and then they were drawing level with the business units opposite the church.

There didn't seem to be many people around. A cat jumped up on to a wall and startled Cassidy and a woman came out on to a doorstep to deposit an empty milk bottle; otherwise the road was deserted.

'This was Grandad's mill, you know,' Leslie announced.

'Yes, I know. Mam told me all about it.'

'Did she?' His eyebrows rose. 'Quite a thriving community when the mill was in full swing. Now a lot of the people who live here are comers-in. People with plenty of money looking for somewhere rural to live. Of course, I can't say anything about that. I live in a rural village myself. A bit more remote than Berrybridge though. Right out in the wilds. You must come and see my house whilst you're here.'

She noticed a painted sign outside one of the units. *Motorbike Museum.* There was a list of times it was open.

'A museum!' she cried.

'Well, sort of,' Leslie said. 'It isn't really a museum because Bryan Enfield sells bikes as well as shows them. Buys them cheap and does them up. Mind you, he has some good models, I'm not saying he hasn't. Are you interested in motorbikes, Cassidy?'

'I don't think so.' She smiled at him.

'Neither am I. I mean, I wouldn't want to own one. Noisy, smelly, dangerous things. I prefer my car. I buy a new one every year.'

Good for you, Cassidy thought whilst saying politely, 'Really?'

Leslie nodded. 'I need to project a good image in my line of work,' he said. 'Taking prospective buyers to see properties, that sort of thing.'

He became launched on what seemed to be his favourite topic—himself. Cassidy was content to walk along at his side, looking at her surroundings, taking it all in so that when she got a chance to come out by herself it would seem familiar to her.

She was just admiring a particularly attractive little house with roses growing round the door and a tiny garden amassed with bright flowers, when she heard Leslie say, 'He's a case in point.'

'Pardon?' Leslie appeared to have switched topics and Cassidy had no idea what he was talking about.

'Bryan Enfield. He's a typical comer-in.' So they were back to the motorbike museum again. 'He's been here a couple of years. Doesn't come from Yorkshire. I believe he hails from Norfolk or some such place. Got a funny accent anyway.'

Not as funny as hers, Cassidy expected.

'Do you know him?' she asked, seeing they were approaching a bend where there stood a nice-looking pub with tables outside.

'Well, he isn't a particular friend of mine, if that's what you mean,' Leslie told her, 'but I know him, yes. A rather clever know-all. Pleased with himself. You know the sort.'

She was certainly beginning to. Leslie, it seemed to her, fitted into that category rather well. It was early to make judgements but she didn't really like him.

'I say,' he suddenly said, 'how about stopping for a drink? I could murder a pint.' He pointed to The Bridge public house.

Cassidy shook her head. 'No, thank you. I'm rather tired. I think I'd like to go back now, if you don't mind. It's been a very long day for me.'

His disappointment was obvious and Cassidy realised Leslie Hawthorn was a person used to getting his own way.

'Suit yourself,' he said, and turning on his heel he started back the way they had come, striding out; Cassidy had almost to run to keep up with him. By the time they reached Berry House, however, his dazzling smile was back.

'I've been longing to meet you, Cassidy,' he
37

said, putting his arm around her shoulders. She steeled herself not to pull away from him. 'I've always known I had relatives in Ireland but it was only lately that Grandad started to talk about you. Were you surprised when he invited you over here?'

'Yes.' Surprised was putting it mildly.

Leslie gave her shoulders an intimate squeeze. 'Don't be put off by the old man's ways. He's got a heart of gold. He'll do anything for me and I expect he will for you when you get to know him better. He's loaded, you know, and we're his only close-living relatives. Did you know your mother had a sister and a brother?'

'Yes, I know a little about them.'

'They're both long gone.' His voice was cold and matter-of-fact and Cassidy's dislike of him was increased. 'James got killed in a riding accident when he was twenty and Esther— well, nobody knows just what became of her, but she was the black sheep of the family. Got herself in the family way and brought disgrace on the old man. People weren't as tolerant twenty odd years ago. He kicked her out.'

She and my mother both, Cassidy thought with a pang of sadness, wondering seriously as Leslie spoke if she could possibly like her grandfather, if there was indeed anything to like about him.

Leslie went on. 'Yes, Esther just disappeared off the face of the earth!'

38

How callous he was. How indifferent to people's feelings and emotions. She wished passionately at that moment that she had never come here. She didn't want to be part of such a family.

'Still,' Leslie spoke cheerfully, 'that's all in the past and doesn't really concern you and me, does it?'

She looked at him. His expression was bland as though they had just been discussing the weather.

'You know a lot about them,' she remarked.

'Ah, well, you see, I ask questions and I keep my eyes and ears open. You'll find you'll need to, because Grandad won't tell you much off his own bat. You'll have to fish for it.'

The idea horrified her. She was a guest in her grandfather's house. She did not want to hear about his children, her aunt and uncle, because she was dreadfully afraid if she learned any more she would begin to hate and despise Matthew Hawthorn. What was the matter with people? First her mother had mentioned the fact of her grandfather's wealth. Now Leslie was positively gloating over it. A thought struck Cassidy. Surely, oh, surely, Grandad didn't think she was here because she was interested in his money?

She nearly blurted out to Leslie that she didn't want anything to do with anything of Matthew's, but she held back. It would be beneath her to even mention such a subject.

39

She would have to be very, very careful how she talked to Leslie. She didn't trust him one inch.

When they reached the doorstep she hoped he would go straight to his car, but instead he followed her up the steps and stood with his arm still around her shoulders in the open doorway. At least it did not seem as though Mrs Dawson had gone to bed yet.

'You're very pretty, Cassidy,' Leslie said and now his voice had taken on a completely different inflexion, one that put Cassidy instantly on her guard. She stood rigid and said nothing. He moved closer to her, bending forward, trying to kiss her on the mouth. She pulled free angrily.

'No!' she cried.

He straightened up but didn't release his hold on her.

'I only want to give you a good-night kiss,' he said innocently. 'Or a welcome to the family kiss.'

Cassidy freed herself from his arms. 'No, I don't want you to.'

His eyes narrowed unpleasantly. 'Oh, come on Cassidy. Don't tell me nobody's tried to kiss you before? A pretty girl like you?'

'Of course they have!' She spoke defensively, her fingers crossed behind her back. Once Sean Reilly had kissed her behind the girls' toilets at school when she was fifteen and she had been out a few times with Mark Corrigan. They had

40

kissed. But she had liked Mark Corrigan. She was not about to let Leslie Hawthorn kiss her. No way.

'So? Why not me?'

'No, Leslie.'

'Oh, dear, and I thought we were going to be friends!' He sighed.

'So we shall be.' How she wished she had not said that. Give him an inch and he would probably take a mile.

Her answer apparently pleased him because his smile came back.

'Then I'll see you later,' he promised, touching her cheek in an oddly intimate way that disturbed her. 'I'll be round tomorrow night. Mrs Dawson makes some lovely bread and cakes and I like to pop in regularly if only to sample them. A lonely bachelor living on his own, you know. Not that I can't cook and fend for myself. I'm a wizard. Grandad said I was to make myself available to you. Show you around. He's a bit past that sort of thing. Can you dance?'

The question surprised her. 'Not very well,' she said.

'Probably just need some practice. Anybody can disco dance, especially with a figure like yours. I'll take you out on the town on Saturday night.'

Not if I can help it, Cassidy thought, especially when I've to be up early for Mass. She wondered what Leslie would say to that.

41

He must know she was a Roman Catholic and she could imagine his lip curling as though she was a religious nutcase.

Eventually he left her and Cassidy closed the door firmly without waiting to see him leave. She hurried up to her room. She was shaking. How stupid! He had only tried to kiss her, but she couldn't help it. She didn't like him and she knew with a terrible hopeless certainty that he was going to be around as much as he possibly could.

CHAPTER FOUR

The sound of bird song awoke Cassidy next morning. As this often happened at home, for a moment she was disorientated and looked around the unfamiliar room in alarm.

Then she remembered. This was not her own bedroom. It was over twice as big for a start and had old-fashioned wallpaper with a big smudgy looking flower pattern, whereas her own room was decorated in sunny yellow and white.

Cassidy got out of bed and kneeled to say her morning prayers. She didn't pray every morning; sometimes she was in too much of a hurry, but today she prayed for the strength to get through this first day. She also prayed that Leslie would not come near the place. He had said he would, but Cassidy was willing to put her faith in the blessed saints!

She went to the bathroom and then got dressed in a pair of white trousers and a pink T-shirt. When she pulled back the bedroom curtains the sun was shining brightly causing flickering patches of brightness in the wood. She would go for another walk this morning, she promised herself. And this time alone. But first she must ask Mrs Dawson for details about St Joseph's church. She didn't want to leave it too late, otherwise she would begin to panic and worry that she wasn't going to get there. To miss Mass was a sin and besides she wanted to go and would be miserable for the rest of her stay here if she didn't.

It was quiet as she went downstairs. Perhaps her grandfather hadn't got up yet. It was only half past eight. Cassidy had slept well, despite her misgivings and surprisingly had found the room quite cool.

She found the kitchen, following the sound of much activity and the appetising smell of frying bacon. Mrs Dawson was setting the big, square table in the middle of the room. The kitchen overlooked the wood, too, and a small rear courtyard. On the wide, tiled windowsill a big black and white cat lay sunning itself.

'Good-morning, Cassidy,' Mrs Dawson greeted. 'Did you sleep well?'

'Oh, yes, thank you.' She crossed to the cat and stroked it. It purred rhythmically in

43

appreciation.

'That's Barnaby. You'll be his friend for life if you make a fuss of him.' Mrs Dawson smiled. She was wearing a large, white apron over her navy-blue dress this morning.

'Do you have a dog?' Cassidy asked.

'A dog? We did have a long time ago, but he had to be put to sleep. Old age and various things wrong with him, poor soul. Your grandad was quite upset but too old to take on another dog, he said. I expect he was right.'

Cassidy smiled shyly. 'I miss my dog,' she said.

'And I'm sure he misses you. Now do you like bacon and eggs, love?'

Cassidy nodded eagerly, feeling she could eat a horse.

'Then it'll be ready in two shakes. Your grandad doesn't get up till about ten. He doesn't eat a proper breakfast these days, though I remember a time when he could eat enough for ten men, and come back for more.'

Cassidy sat at the table. 'He's very fit for his age, though, isn't he?'

'He can't grumble, that's for sure.' Mrs Dawson took a warmed plate from the rack above the cooker. 'Though if you ask me he doesn't get out nearly enough. He's got a gammy leg, you see, a relic of the last war; it's never been right since. Gives him quite a bit of pain sometimes, but he bears it all with fortitude.'

She smiled broadly as she set the plate of bacon and eggs before Cassidy. It looked very tasty. 'Well, love, now you're here p'raps your grandad'll get out a bit more often. Show you around. Not that he has any transport, but there's buses and taxis, so I always tell him.'

Cassidy picked up her knife and fork. 'Leslie said Grandad wanted him to show me round.'

Mrs Dawson made a snorting sort of noise. 'It'd be Leslie who suggested it, you mark my words. He likes to put ideas in the old man's head. There was a time when I first came here, when young Leslie's parents were still alive, they were always dumping him on your grandad. Ay, and on me as well. Bossy little boy he was. Rude, too. I smacked his bare legs for him more than once.' She winked at Cassidy and Cassidy glowed inside when she realised she had a very good friend in Mrs Dawson, who obviously thought the same as she did about Leslie Hawthorn.

'Did you find out about St Joseph's for me, Mrs Dawson?' she asked politely as she started her breakfast.

'Oh, ay, I'm glad you mentioned it.' Mrs Dawson took a folded piece of paper out of her apron pocket. 'It's got all the details of the Masses and the bus times. You can catch a bus the other side of the bridge; that's the main road into town, though I expect you came that way yesterday.'

Cassidy said she had.

45

'The bus station is only a short walk from St Joseph's church, so you can't go wrong. The only thing is, there's no bus before eight o'clock on a Sunday so you'll miss the early Mass. Will that bother you?'

'Oh, no,' Cassidy said. 'It's very kind of you, Mrs Dawson.' She put the paper in her pocket to study later. 'Where did you get the information from?'

'Oh, I made a couple of phone calls,' was all Mrs Dawson would admit to.

Yes, definitely a great ally, Cassidy reiterated, tucking heartily into the plate of food.

*   *   *

She insisted on helping with the washing up and she made her own bed before leaving the house. She told Mrs Dawson she was going for a walk and wouldn't be long and was given a cheery wave of farewell. Cassidy set off with a light step. It was a glorious morning. Could the good weather possibly last? There seemed to be a bit more activity this morning. Women doing their shopping; cars passing along the road, though not too many of those; a milk float going by with a whistling young man in a blue overall who bid her, 'Good-morning.'

She decided to walk in the opposite direction to that she and Leslie had taken the previous evening. This way, she felt certain, would lead

46

her round to the wood at the back of Berry House. She passed a row of terrace houses and one small shop, which displayed wool, knitting patterns and the like in its window.

Then she came to a small, cobbled street, rather quaint with other small houses on either side. They had no gardens and their bright painted front doors opened directly on to the cobbles. Some had pots of flowers or potted plants stood under the small, low-set windows. Cassidy could imagine that in the days of Hawthorn's mill, these houses would belong to the millworkers, perhaps to people who were very poor, especially back in the Thirties and Forties when the mill was a going concern and probably the main, if not the only, employer in the district.

Now the houses had a look of wealth about them. Shiny door knockers, double-glazed windows. One had its door open and Cassidy could see the smart parquet flooring in the entrance. One even had a 'For Sale' sign in the window. The name of the estate agents was Hawthorn & Moffatt. Leslie's firm. She wondered how much the asking price was. Not cheap, that was for certain.

Seeing the sign brought Leslie back into her mind. He was sure to turn up that evening, all smiles, until, of course, she said something he didn't like. She hoped he would get the message that she wasn't interested in him, otherwise things could be unpleasant.

47

There was the wood, up a slight incline and beyond a small gate set in a low, stone wall. It could not be a private wood, as there was no sign to that effect and, tossing thoughts of Leslie aside, Cassidy quickened her footsteps. She calculated that if she walked to the left she would presently pass along the back of her grandfather's house, but she didn't want to make her way back yet awhile, so she set a course straight ahead of her, going deeper into the wood, which wasn't very big and wasn't dense either.

It was quiet and pleasant in the wood, the grass springy and soft beneath her feet. There was something about a wood that made her feel serene and composed. Whatever the season of the year, a wood had something to offer. Blue-bells in spring, crisp, rustling leaves in autumn, fairy-tale snow or frost patterns in winter and now, in the middle of summer, a shady glen where the sun made dappled patterns and birds sang around her.

Into this friendly silence came the sound of a dog barking and the thud-thud of its feet as it bounded through the trees. It might be a big dog from the sound of it. Cassidy wasn't worried. She liked big dogs. This one turned out to be a red setter, with a rich, glossy coat, feathery tail, dark eyes. As soon as it saw Cassidy, it lolloped towards her and she bent to pat it.

'Hello, there,' she said. 'Now aren't you a

beauty?'

The dog's owner was not far behind.

'Amber!' he called out and the dog responded at once, rushing back to his side.

'Good-morning,' Cassidy greeted. 'I was just admiring your dog.'

In any other circumstances she would have been horribly tongue-tied and gauche upon meeting a stranger, especially a man, but a dog created a common ground, a topic for conversation.

'She's a bit silly at the moment, I'm afraid,' the man said. 'She's still only very young.' He swung the lead he carried gently to and fro.

He was tall and well-built with dark brown hair that curled boyishly, though Cassidy guessed he must be in his late twenties at least. He had a friendly face, an open face. He was wearing dark blue overalls as though going to or from some place of work. He wasn't a local man; he had an accent that Cassidy could not place.

'I haven't seen you in here before,' the man remarked, seeming to eye her keenly, 'and I come in here with Amber nearly every day.'

'No, I'm a visitor, staying with my grandfather for a couple of weeks.'

He smiled. 'From Ireland by the sound of it.'

Cassidy pulled a face. 'Is it so obvious?'

'I'm afraid so.'

'Ah, but you must be a visitor, too,' Cassidy said, 'because you don't have a Yorkshire

49

accent either.'

'Guilty.' He held up his hands in mock surrender. 'I'm from Norfolk.'

Of course. Bryan Enfield. She nearly said the name aloud but if she had done, he would have wanted to know how she knew and that would mean mentioning Leslie. The least said about Leslie the better.

'But I do live here,' he went on. 'Not quite accepted as a local but getting there slowly but surely.' He grinned. He had lovely, white teeth and his dark, greyish blue eyes crinkled at the corners.

'Well, I'd better get on with my walk,' Cassidy said.

'And I'll take Amber home. Perhaps we might meet again, Miss...' His voice rose in query.

'O'Connor. Cassidy O'Connor.'

'*Very* Irish.' His voice was teasing, but she didn't seem to mind.

'And what's your name?'

'Enfield. Bryan. I keep the motorbike museum. Have you seen it?'

'Only from the outside.'

'Come along one day and I'll show you around. Even if you don't know the first thing about motorbikes I'm sure you'll find it interesting.'

Cassidy smiled. 'I might just do that.'

He lifted his hand in a gesture of farewell, whistled to his dog and walked off in the opposite direction. When Cassidy had gone a fair distance she turned round but Bryan Enfield and Amber had disappeared.

So that was the 'comer-in' as Leslie had described him. The man who was clever, and pleased with himself. He didn't appear to be that sort of person at all. He came across to Cassidy as easy-going and friendly. Any man who had such a beautiful dog must be all right. She was just willing to bet that Leslie Hawthorn had no pet of any sort to share his ultra-modern house!

When she got back to the house, her grandfather was up, standing in the open doorway, leaning on his stick. He could have been admiring his garden or he could have been keeping an eye out for her. He waved his stick as she came through the gateway.

'Had a nice stroll?' he called.

'Lovely, thank you. I've been in the wood. It's so peaceful in there.'

'My word, it's many a long day since I strolled through that wood.'

Shyly Cassidy said, 'You could go with me, Grandad. You could hold on to me.'

He gave a loud, amused laugh. 'A big chap like me leaning on a scrap like you? I don't think so.'

Matthew turned and walked slowly back along the hallway, Cassidy following. It was cool and dim inside; the sun had not yet reached the front of the house.

51

'By the way,' her grandfather began, 'young Leslie's phoned. He won't be coming round tonight. He's got to show some fellow round a property. A big wig from the sound of it so Leslie didn't want to put him off. He says he'll be here tomorrow night without fail.'

He needn't rush, Cassidy thought, though grateful for tonight's reprieve. Matthew sat in his own high-backed chair, resting his walking-stick between his legs. Cassidy sat on the couch looking out of the window. There was a good view of the church from this room. She could not quite see the industrial units opposite, not without craning her neck. She wondered if Bryan Enfield was at his museum now.

'Would you like to phone your mother?' her grandfather asked suddenly.

Cassidy looked at him. 'We don't have a phone,' she said. 'But I could perhaps phone the post office. I work there and if I could give Mrs Mulligan your number, Mam could ring me back.'

'Fine. Fine.' He drummed his fingers on the chair arm, humming quietly. He had large, gnarled hands with blunt fingers. Cassidy noticed he wore a wide, gold wedding ring. She did not know much about her grandmother, Matthew's wife, who had died the year after her mother, the youngest of the three Hawthorn children, was born.

Elizabeth Hawthorn, according to Mary O'Connor's limited knowledge had fallen

52

victim to a flu epidemic in 1948 at the age of twenty-seven. Matthew had been a widower for forty-three years. What a great pity that over the years he had not been able to draw comfort from his two surviving children instead of driving them both away.

Leslie had told her Matthew's only son, James, had died in a riding accident. So her grandfather had been left with nobody in the end; nobody to love or to love him. Was his real reason for sending for her to make up for this tragic waste of time? He seemed close to Leslie and surely he must realise that Leslie had many faults and was not, quite frankly, very likeable. Well, now he had her, Cassidy, and she would do all in her power to make him happy and proud of her.

His voice broke in on her thoughts.

'How is your mother, Cassidy?'

She was taken aback by the question and she stammered out the answer. 'She ... she's very well, thank you.'

'It can't have been easy for her.'

'No.'

They were silent for a few moments. Cassidy wanted to come right out and ask him why he had cut himself adrift from Mary, but she daren't. It wasn't the right moment. Maybe later when they were both much surer of each other, but it was as though her grandfather was able to read her thoughts.

He said, in his blunt outspoken way, 'It was

53

all a long time ago, lass. So long ago that I can't remember it very clearly. She was a headstrong girl, your mother, far and away the wildest of the three of them. He wasn't good enough for her. Did he provide for the two of you, eh? Did he treat your mother well?'

Cassidy spoke in a whisper. 'If you're talking about my father, he died before I was born.' She had already reminded her grandfather of this fact.

He shocked her when he slammed his hand down angrily on the chair's wooden arm.

'Couldn't he keep going long enough to be any use to Mary?'

To Cassidy it seemed a terrible thing to say.

They were on dangerous ground. Cassidy did not know how much her grandfather knew about his daughter's life with Patrick O'Connor. There were undoubtedly many things he could tell her, but as he had just said, it all happened a long time ago. Did she really want to resurrect the old ghosts, the old hurts? Leslie had told her her grandfather would be close-mouthed about the past. It did not seem so to Cassidy. She was certain she could get him to tell her plenty if she wanted to, but she didn't.

However, there was something she would like to know and she asked him now, whilst he was in a confiding frame of mind. 'Do you have any photographs, Grandad?'

'Photographs? Ay, scores of 'em. Had you

54

any particular ones in mind?'

'Old ones. I'd like to see my grandmother. And Mam, of course.'

He eased himself out of his chair. His voice was particularly gruff. 'I'll get Mrs Dawson to ferret out all the albums. I don't know where they are, but don't expect me to sit with you, mewling over 'em.' With that he walked straight-backed out of the room.

Cassidy knew she had touched a raw nerve and she only hoped she hadn't set her relationship with her grandfather back a hundred years.

*   *   *

Her meeting with Bryan Enfield in the wood next morning was not accidental. She had been looking out for him and Amber, and when they met up, they walked along together. Cassidy felt perfectly at ease with this quiet-spoken, friendly man. It was like meeting a friend when she saw him coming towards her between the trees and Amber ran to greet her.

'Who needs to go abroad,' Bryan said, 'with weather like this?'

'It was the same in Ireland,' Cassidy told him.

He looked at her with mock disbelief. 'Now I can't believe that. It rains all the time, surely.'

Cassidy laughed. 'No, it does not.'

'Coming to see my museum this morning?'

55

His voice was casual as he threw a stick for Amber.

'Yes, I'd like to.'

'I'll take Amber along. Sometimes she stays with me all day.' He winked. 'As a guard dog!'

'Never!' Cassidy cried, ruffling the dog's long, silky ears.

They kept their walk in the wood short. As they walked past Berry House towards the bike museum, Cassidy nearly said, 'That's where I'm staying. That's my grandfather's house,' but she didn't. For some reason she wasn't sure of, she didn't want Bryan to know who she was. It wasn't a rational decision, just a feeling she had.

Bryan unlocked the heavy, brown-painted door to the museum and stepped aside for her to enter before him.

'I usually charge admission,' he said, 'but I'll waive the fee in your case.'

'Do you have many people coming?' Cassidy felt sure that in a small village like Berrybridge there wouldn't be the call for a place of this kind.

'Oh, you'd be surprised. If you're around here long enough, you'll hear them as they're usually on motor-bikes.' He leaned towards her and whispered hoarsely, 'Hell's Angels!'

'Really?'

'Cross my heart. They tear up the village and rape and pillage.' His face was perfectly solemn.

56

Cassidy laughed and gave him a shove. That's how much at ease she felt with Bryan Enfield.

The inside of the museum was fascinating. In what had formerly been a huge mill shed with skylight windows, the various motorcycles were displayed in roped-off sections. Immediately on entry was a glass-partitioned office. Amber went straight into the office and flopped down on an old rug which was obviously hers. As Cassidy walked round looking at the bikes, Bryan told her something about each one of them.

They all looked brand new to Cassidy but were not new, far from it, only lovingly and painstakingly restored. She knew nothing at all about motor-bikes but listening to Bryan she realised he lived and breathed them.

'This is a Velocette,' he said, pointing to one enormous black machine. 'See the fishtail exhaust. That was its hallmark.'

'It's beautiful!' Cassidy sighed. 'Look at the lettering. Did you do that?' The name *Velocette* was intricately painted in scroll-type golden letters.

'Alas no. My skills don't stretch to art work.'

Cassidy pointed to the next bike.

'Royal Enfield. That's your name.'

'Merely a coincidence,' Bryan assured her.

There were so many bikes with so many names including a BSA wartime dispatch bike, painted in camouflage colours, and a Norton

Dominator in bright, gleaming red. Leading off the main display hall was a workshop littered with bits and pieces, machinery and partly-restored bikes.

'Do you work here by yourself?' Cassidy asked, itching to touch one of the gleaming machines, to smooth her hand across its sparkling chrome, or the leather of a seat, but not daring to. She had had no idea that the motorcycle was such a beautiful object.

'I have a friend who shares the business with me, fifty-fifty,' Bryan told her.

How much nicer that sounded than the way Leslie had described his own business colleague. 'I have a junior partner, but he's merely learning the ropes, a general dogsbody really. I'm the one in charge, though.'

'Where do all the bikes come from?'

'Here and there. As I said we have a lot of interested enthusiasts who visit us and we get information from them. We buy and sell as well as display.' Bryan looked at his watch. 'Well, I'll be due to open in twenty minutes. Are you going to stay on a while?'

Cassidy wanted to but felt she had been away from the house for long enough.

'I think I'd better go. My grandfather was still in bed when I left.' She waited for Bryan to ask about her grandfather, but he didn't. He merely said, 'How about letting me take you for a spin tonight?'

'On a motor-bike?' she asked.

'Naturally. I don't have a car.'

'One of these?'

'Oh, no, I have my own. I've got a spare crash helmet and all I ask is that you wear trousers and sensible shoes.'

Cassidy nodded eagerly. 'I'd love to,' she said. Remembering almost at once that Leslie was due to come round that evening. 'Could we meet early? Say around six thirty? Would that be convenient?' she suggested.

Bryan nodded. 'Fine. Whatever you say.'

They arranged that Cassidy would come to the museum. She knew Bryan lived in Berrybridge but she did not know where. She said goodbye to Amber who wagged her tail eagerly and left the building, going out into the warm sunshine.

She felt excited by the prospect of seeing Bryan socially and taking her first ride on a motor-bike.

CHAPTER FIVE

She confided in Mrs Dawson, but decided not to mention her trip out to her grandfather. She had a feeling he would not approve, especially when he had been the one to tell her Leslie was coming. Mrs Dawson, not being too enamoured of half-cousin Leslie, was quite happy to aid and abet Cassidy in a little bit of

59

subterfuge.

'I'll give you a front door key,' she said conspiratorially, 'and you'd best keep it while you're here.'

'What will you tell Grandad?' Cassidy asked.

'I'll say you've got a date. As soon as you've finished your tea, you get yourself ready and off. I'll have great pleasure in telling young Leslie you've gone out, though not who with, of course.'

Mrs Dawson knew Bryan Enfield only by sight, but declared he looked a nice, young man, and that he had a lovely dog. Cassidy could not agree more.

As she started out of the kitchen where she had been speaking to Mrs Dawson, the housekeeper said, 'Your grandad mentioned the photo albums, love. I'm going to look them out when I get a moment.'

'Thanks,' Cassidy said, 'but there's no hurry.'

There was the phone call home to think about as well, but not just yet. She had already written a letter to her mother, posting it the previous afternoon. The day passed slowly for Cassidy and she could not keep at bay a feeling of guilt because she was keeping something from her grandfather. She managed though and when, as she left the tea table, he reminded her of Leslie's visit, she pretended she hadn't heard him, hurrying through the door as fast as she could go.

It proved to be a case of actually sneaking out of the house and this did not improve Cassidy's guilty conscience, but once she was hurrying along the road, all she could think of was seeing Bryan again. He was waiting for her, wearing motor-bike gear, with two crash helmets on the saddle of the enormous black bike.

'My goodness!' Cassidy cried.

'What's the matter?' Bryan asked. 'You're not getting cold feet, I hope.'

'A little nervous maybe,' Cassidy admitted.

'Climb aboard.' Bryan gestured gallantly. 'Cling on to me and you'll be as safe as houses.'

'Don't go too fast, will you?' Cassidy pleaded.

He handed her the smaller of the two crash helmets.

'Where to, madam? The world is your oyster.'

Cassidy had already decided where she wanted to go if it was possible.

'How far is it to Haworth?' she asked quickly.

'Haworth as in Jane Eyre?'

Cassidy nodded.

'OK, Haworth it shall be.'

Cassidy was so excited she nearly did a little dance. She could hardly believe it. It was only her second day in Berrybridge and already one of her dreams was coming true. Added to this

61

was the wonderful feeling of being with Bryan, whom she really liked and trusted instinctively and implicitly. Once on the back of the bike, clinging on to him for grim death, breathing in the scent of his leather jacket, feeling the strength and broadness of his back, Cassidy scarcely had time to think of anything.

It was quite a while before she ventured to open her eyes and when she did she wished she hadn't. They seemed to be travelling at an alarming speed, houses, streets, shops whizzing by. It was a great comfort to Cassidy to have Bryan in front of her.

They left the town behind and travelled for a while on a motorway which was more hair-raising than ever, but when the scenery began to change, to become wilder and more dramatic, Cassidy felt brave enough to raise her head a little and look where they were going.

Why, this was wonderful! Exhilarating! Sensations she had never before experienced were coursing through her body. The air whipped coldly against her face and she was glad of her thick sweater and jeans.

Occasionally, Bryan glanced back at her, grinning through the visor of his helmet, but it was impossible to talk and for the most part he kept his eyes firmly on the road ahead.

Cassidy saw the sign for Haworth, pointing to it eagerly, grabbing Bryan's shoulder to draw his attention to it. He nodded and followed the sign. First they went down a very steep hill and almost immediately they were going up another hill. Fields and moors, wild and gaunt, surrounded them. The views were breathtaking on such a lovely summer evening.

The bike slowed down as Bryan turned into a big carpark opposite a war memorial. He removed his helmet and Cassidy did the same, shaking out her short hair.

'Welcome to Haworth,' Bryan said. 'We've a few minutes walk from here. All up hill, I'm afraid, but it'll be well worth it. The shops are bound to be open and the Bronte Museum, too.'

He helped her off the bike and for a moment he held her in his arms, looking into her eyes. She felt good.

*　　*　　*

Cassidy could never remember enjoying herself so much. Bryan was a wonderful companion. Generous, too. He insisted on paying the entry fee into the museum, an experience Cassidy would not have missed for the world. Before that they had walked the length of Haworth's main street, browsing in the little crowded shops where even Cassidy had to lower her head to enter. After being presented with a handmade, embroidered cushion, a small, grey felt mouse in a bridal outfit and a blue, glass pig, Cassidy dared

63

scarcely look at anything else, but it was hard not to, the shops were so fascinating.

They had tea and scones in a quaint tea shop and looked round the churchyard, reading the ancient gravestones, pondering over the people buried there as some of the graves were very old.

The evening went by so quickly. They managed to go for a walk beyond the museum along a deserted road with only an occasional house or farm, then Bryan suggested they had better start for home.

'I'd like to take you for a drink when we get back,' he said. 'We can't go before that as I'm driving.'

That sounded to Cassidy like the perfect end to a perfect evening and made the parting from Haworth so much easier. Now she had more confidence on the bike and enjoyed the long ride home. It was getting close to ten o'clock when they reached Berrybridge. The sun had set and the night air felt like velvet. They went to The Bridge Inn, sitting at one of the tables outside. Cassidy had some misgivings about being spotted by Leslie, but she was willing to risk it. After all, she would have to face him some time.

Whilst they sat they each talked about themselves. Cassidy told Bryan about her mother, her dog, her job at the post office. She said she was staying with her grandfather who was practically a stranger to her. She said she

64

was very happy in Berrybridge, but she did not say that Bryan was the chief cause of her happiness.

Bryan in his turn told her both his parents were dead and that he had moved north from Norfolk just over three years ago. He had opened the museum two years ago, fulfilling a long-held dream.

As soon as it became really dark and the tables around them were emptying, Cassidy knew it was time for them to say goodnight, but dreaded the moment of parting. Bryan had put his hand over hers as it rested on the top of the table. She had welcomed the gesture. She knew how it would be all too easy to feel deeply for this man.

He said he would leave his bike parked outside the pub and walk her home. Cassidy felt a moment of panic. What if Leslie should still be there, watching out for her return? She would not put it past him to do so and the last person she wanted to see at that moment was Leslie Hawthorn. Because of this dread she took Bryan on a roundabout route and presently paused outside a small, detached house set back from the road.

'Well, this is it.' She hated the lie she was forced to tell and later, when she told Bryan the truth, she hoped he would understand. He looked at the house which was in darkness, at least at the front and Cassidy had one moment of heart-stopping fear. What if this was

Bryan's own house?

He said, 'Nice place. I must let you see my house some time. That's if you want to see me again?'

'Oh, yes, please!'

He seemed amused by her eagerness. 'Tomorrow?'

'Yes.' Cassidy nodded.

'What time? It will have to be evening, I'm afraid.'

Could she possibly wait so long?

'I'll meet you same time, same place,' she said, 'but I won't have to be late home. I'm going to Mass on Sunday morning.'

'I'll take you on the bike. Which church?'

'St Joseph's near the town centre, but honestly, there's no need. I can catch a bus. It'll be very early.'

'I'll take you,' he said firmly, 'and that's final.'

She did not argue any more. The more time she could spend with Bryan Enfield, the happier she would be.

They were silent for a few moments. When Bryan moved closer and put his arms round her, Cassidy knew he was going to kiss her. She lifted her face to his and accepted his first soft, gentle kiss on her parted lips. Then he drew her even closer and kissed her longer and harder, taking her breath away.

When they parted, he smiled at her.

'You're quite a girl, Cassidy O'Connor,' he

66

said quietly.

She was walking on air. She knew she would never be able to sleep that night and it would have nothing to do with the warm air.

Once Bryan had left her and she hurried towards Berry House she was glad to find Mrs Dawson and her grandfather had gone to bed and that there was no sign of Leslie, either.

She let herself quietly in and tiptoed upstairs, not bothering to put on a light. In her prayers before she got into bed, she gave grateful thanks for her meeting with Bryan and asked humbly that their relationship should continue to blossom.

*   *   *

When Cassidy came downstairs on Saturday morning she was surprised to hear her grandfather's voice coming from the sitting-room. He must have got up earlier than usual. She was sorry, as she had expected to have a little time to collect herself before she faced him. As she reached the hallway, Mrs Dawson came out of the sitting-room, putting her finger to her lips when she saw Cassidy and indicating that she should follow the housekeeper into the kitchen.

Cassidy did so, where Mrs Dawson spoke to her in a hurried whisper.

'He's on the war path this morning. Went on summat terrible when you'd gone out

67

yesterday. Actually I told him you'd met a girl in the village and gone out with her. It seemed better that way. Do you mind?'

'No, of course not.' Cassidy was glad. It would save a lot of awkward questions, but she did wonder at her real reasons for wanting to deceive her grandfather at all. Could it possibly be because she feared he would react towards her exactly as he had to her mother all those years before? Such a reaction, Cassidy knew, would be unfair and unreasonable, but if he was as angry as Mrs Dawson had said...

'Has he eaten breakfast?' Cassidy asked.

'Not enough to keep a sparrow alive, but yes, he has. Sit down, love. I'll get yours.'

'No, I'll see Grandad first. And what about Leslie? Did he turn up?'

Mrs Dawson rolled her eyes heavenward.

'Oh, my, did he? Like a couple of caged lions they were. You'd think they owned you.'

Cassidy went with a feeling of trepidation to face her grandfather. He was standing by the sitting-room window looking out into the street. He turned sharply when she appeared.

'Oh, so you did come back.' He spoke sarcastically.

Cassidy stood her ground. She wasn't feeling very brave but it would not do to let the old man intimidate her.

'I was home before eleven, Grandad,' she told him.

'And where did you go?'

'A walk. And for a drink.'

'Just you and another girl into a public house?'

Cassidy had to laugh at that. 'Grandad, I'm over twenty-one. I am quite capable of looking after myself,' she said lightly.

'You're my responsibility, young woman, while you're under my roof. Have the goodness to keep me informed of your movements in future.'

'Yes. I'm sorry,' Cassidy mumbled.

'I think you ought to apologise to Leslie, as well,' Matthew went on. 'You made him look a right fool.'

Cassidy felt a surge of anger. She wasn't having that!

'Why did I?' She shot at him.

He moved to sit in his high-backed chair, thudding his stick on to the carpet.

'I told you he was coming to see you, didn't I?'

'You told me he was coming, yes, but not necessarily to see me.'

The old man's eyes flashed angrily and Cassidy could see what a terrifying man he must have been when he was younger.

'Don't split hairs, Cassidy,' he barked. 'The lad's fair smitten with you. If you knew how he'd been looking forward to you coming here. He's a fine, upstanding, young man. He's got his own business, I expect he's told you already. He's going places and he'll come into a

69

tidy sum when I go.' He paused dramatically. 'And so will you. There's just the two of you. It'll all be yours one day. Yours and Leslie's.'

So her mother had been right. Now it was said and out in the open. Cassidy sat down abruptly and her grandfather gave a harsh laugh.

'I can see that's knocked the stuffing out of you,' he said. 'Well, I'm not sorry I've told you, though I was hoping to tell you in a bit of a different way. I wanted to meet you and I wasn't disappointed when I did, but if you're going to be as headstrong and wilful as that blessed mother of yours, well...' He paused again. 'I'm just warning you, that's all.'

Cassidy was trembling but with rage not fear. How dare he threaten her, for that's what he was doing. She took a few deep breaths, holding her tongue when what she really wanted to do was yell and shout at him and tell him what he could do with his money, but she must not. He was an old man and she had been brought up to respect the elderly. After a couple of moments' silence, so quiet that they could hear Mrs Dawson rattling pots and pans in the kitchen, and the ponderous ticking of the grandfather clock in the hall, Matthew said in a completely different voice, loud and jovial!

'Oh, go on with you. Go and get your breakfast and think on. Don't do another disappearing act. You're not on a chain and you don't have to clock in and out, but just try

70

to be considerate, that's all I ask.'

Cassidy scurried away. When she reached the kitchen and saw Mrs Dawson's anxious expression she let out a large, exaggerated sigh.

'As bad as that, was it?' Mrs Dawson said.

'Worse,' Cassidy groaned.

'Here's your breakfast!' A plateful of bacon and egg was set down on the table. Cassidy was ravenous. As she started to eat, she glanced at the kitchen clock. Now she would have missed Bryan and Amber on their daily walk round the wood. And it was over eight hours to their evening date!

Cassidy's ordeal was not over. Later in the day she had to face Leslie, as well.

She had managed to put through a phone call to Mrs Mulligan and within half an hour of doing so her mother had phoned her back. They chatted for quite some time. Cassidy said how much she was enjoying herself but carefully avoided mentioning either Bryan or her 'words' with her grandfather that morning. Her mother asked a lot of questions and Cassidy was glad to answer them all. She could tell her mother was pleased.

Cassidy asked after Murphy and was told he was fit and well though still going into her bedroom every morning to wake her up and showing great concern when she wasn't there.

'Poor Murphy!' Cassidy sympathised.

'You'll be going to Mass tomorrow?' Mary asked.

'Of course,' Cassidy said.

'Good girl!'

The phone call over, Cassidy went back to her room deciding to keep a low profile for the rest of the morning. It was a bit overcast today, so the sunshine wasn't there to entice her out of doors. She washed her hair and wrote another letter home, though found it a bit hard to know what to put, having exhausted every topic on the phone.

Later she read a magazine she had bought on her journey and never finished. She heard Mrs Dawson vacuuming downstairs and what she presumed were her grandfather's heavy footsteps coming upstairs, but very little else.

Presently she lay back on her bed and gave her dreamy thoughts over to Bryan and the wonderful evening they would be spending together. What would they do? Where would they go? Would she, should she, go to his house? Would he kiss her again? *Am I falling in love with Bryan Enfield?*

This last question came as a surprise and caused Cassidy to open her eyes wide and sit upright on the bed.

Of course she wasn't; she couldn't be. Could she? Love at first sight; that did not happen in real life. She was allowing her imagination to run away with her. After all, she was far from experienced in such matters. Bryan was charming. He had showed her attention, he had kissed her, but...

A knock on the bedroom door startled her. 'Yes?' she called out.

'It's me, love,' Mrs Dawson said. 'Leslie's here. He wants to see you.'

Cassidy came down to earth with a bump. 'Coming,' she called out.

Leslie was waiting in the sitting-room. He was alone. Cassidy remembered her grandfather going upstairs earlier, possibly for a nap. Leslie was wearing a blue and white striped, short-sleeved shirt and light grey trousers. He looked like someone from a mail order catalogue. Every hair in place; knife-like creases in his trousers; expensive-looking, soft-leather shoes. He was not pleased and for once Cassidy was not subjected to his dazzling smile. He did not get up when she entered and smugly she thought his manners did not match the perfection of his immaculate looks.

'Hello, Leslie,' she greeted him cheerfully.

He came straight to the point. 'Where were you last night?'

'Out.' She sat as far away from him as possible.

'I know that.' He sounded impatient. 'Gone out with a girlfriend, so Mrs Dawson told me. What girlfriend? Where did you meet her?'

'What is this? Am I on trial?' Cassidy tried to keep her voice light, but she was getting a little tired of being grilled, first by her grandfather, now by Leslie.

'I said I'd be coming to take you out,' Leslie

73

grumbled. 'I had the evening all planned. Tickets for the disco. Everything. I feel most let down.'

'Well, I'm sorry your evening was spoiled,' Cassidy began but Leslie cut in.

'Oh, it wasn't, don't go running away with the idea that I moped all night on your account.'

'I'm glad to hear it.' Cassidy spoke quietly.

He got up then and came to stand by her, looking down at her, waving his car keys in her face.

'You know, I don't understand you at all,' he told her. 'You come over here, you don't know a living soul and I'm here, offering you friendship, offering to escort you wherever you want to go. My time's important, I'd like you to know. Time's money in my business. You might at least show a little gratitude. And besides, I'm only doing what Grandad wants. He has plans for us, Cassidy. Big plans.'

Cassidy did not like the sound of that. Nor did she like Leslie towering over her. She stood up, so if not exactly on a level with him, she did not feel dwarfed by him.

'Plans?' she repeated suspiciously. 'What sort of plans?'

If he was referring to her grandfather's money she did not want to know any more about that.

'For us. For you and me.'

'I'm not with you.'

74

Leslie heaved a great sigh and spoke slowly and deliberately.

'He wants, he hopes, we'll get married one day and not in the dim and distant future, either. A man turned eighty doesn't have all that much of a future, no matter how lucky he is. I'm only your half-cousin, Cassidy, and I don't mind marrying you if it'll make the old man happy.'

He gave her the first of that day's wonderful smiles whilst she stood there spluttering, trying to find the right words that would finally shut his mouth.

'In fact, I'm quite fond of you. Oh, you need knocking into shape a bit, but that's no problem. You're a good looker. I intend introducing you to all my friends over the week-end. Tonight I've arranged—'

He broke off, his mouth falling open, staring at her in utter disbelief, because about halfway through that pompous, idiotic, ridiculous speech Cassidy had started to laugh and once she started she found it impossible to stop.

'Oh, Leslie, your face!' She collapsed on to the settee, tears rolling down her cheeks. She picked up a cushion and pressed it over her mouth to try to stifle the laughter.

When Leslie snatched the cushion from her and flung it across the room, grabbing her roughly and pulling her to her feet, it did the trick. The laughter ceased immediately but before she could yell at him to let go of her, he was kissing her, grinding his mouth against hers.

She struggled and fought but Leslie was tremendously strong, his strength belying his soft good looks. His hands were against her back, holding her tightly against him. She felt she could not breathe. When he did release her, Cassidy's mouth stung from the pressure of his and she was filled with such a bitter loathing she wanted to kill him. His look was one of triumph.

'That's just a sample, so you'll know I'm not to be trifled with, Cassidy, or laughed at. And, by the way, I enjoyed it very much.'

'Why, you—' Too late, she swung up her hand to smack his stupid, vapid face, but he was too quick for her, stepping nimbly out of the room. Cassidy stood, her heart thumping madly.

When, a moment later, Leslie's face appeared outside the window as he tapped against it and cried out, 'I'll pick you up about eight. Be ready!' Cassidy snatched up the cushion from the floor and flung it ineffectively at the window.

CHAPTER SIX

Cassidy made up her mind that if she was still seeing Bryan on Monday she would tell her

76

grandfather the truth. In the meantime, the imaginary girlfriend would have to come to her rescue again. This time, however, she did not sneak out of the house, but made sure that Matthew knew she was leaving. He stared at her for a moment then, without showing his feelings one way or the other, he nodded. 'Right,' he said, 'enjoy yourself.'

Cassidy sensed he was itching to fire questions at her, but he did not do so. Inevitably he mentioned Leslie.

'Yes, he's coming here, Grandad,' Cassidy told him, 'but I've already said I don't want to go to a disco. I've to be up very early for Mass in the morning.'

'Oh, ay, Mass,' he muttered in a slightly scathing way.

Cassidy thought it wisest not to comment. Nor did she intend telling her grandfather that she knew about his little 'plan' for her and Leslie. The least said about that the better.

As soon as she left the house she had thoughts for no-one but Bryan. She had not seen him all day. He was waiting for her outside the museum. Amber was with him. Sometimes she felt she was running great risks, not only that her grandfather would find her out in a lie but also that Bryan would discover she had deceived him about where she was staying. She was surprising herself by the lengths she was prepared to go to keep secrets. She knew it was a sin to tell lies, even white ones, and could only square it with her conscience by knowing it was only temporary. In a few days time she would know what her feelings were for Bryan and his for her. Then she would not mind the whole world knowing about him!

Because Cassidy did not want to be too late home, they were only going for a walk tonight and Bryan had advised her to wear some sensible shoes, so she had put on the sandals she wore that first night to go for a walk with Leslie. Bryan was wearing dark jeans and a casual shirt. She ran straight into his arms and they kissed. Then they walked along hand-in-hand, Amber plodding at Bryan's side.

'I know where there's a nice pub,' he said, 'but it's a fair walk and involves some climbing. Are you fit?'

Cassidy laughed. 'Of course!'

As they walked along through the village towards the bridge, it was hard to realise they had only met a couple of days before. She felt she had known Bryan all her life. They seemed so right together. He was quiet and liked quiet places, country pubs, walking, dogs—they had so much in common.

He took her now along a narrow lane and over a stile and they proceeded to walk across the fields on a well-worn footpath that wound its way ahead towards higher ground in the distance. Amber bounded ahead, free of the lead. The overcast sky had cleared during the day and it was another pleasant, warm evening. High above, a skylark sang happily.

'There's the pub!' Bryan pointed into the distance. A long, white building was perched on the top of a hill.

'I'll need a drink when we get there,' Cassidy said.

He put his arm comfortably around her shoulders. They paused to kiss. Cassidy had never been so happy.

*   *   *

Over the next two days she and Bryan spent every possible minute together. Only Mrs Dawson knew the truth of where Cassidy was and whom she was with. Cassidy went to Bryan's house which wasn't actually in Berrybridge but some distance outside, but easily walkable from the village. He made her a meal and later they sat on the deep-buttoned couch in the lounge and kissed over and over again. When Amber tried to jump up between them, Bryan laughed loudly.

'She makes a good chaperone, don't you think?' he said, ruffling the dog's glossy coat.

He was joking but secretly Cassidy was glad Amber was there. She was beginning to fall very much in love and it was a completely new experience for her. Emotions were running riot inside her. She wanted to be with Bryan all the time. It was a real effort to part from him when

79

it was time to go home. Sometimes she feared that this bubble of happiness would burst. It was too good. How could it possibly last? Soon she would have to tell her grandfather the truth because she wanted him to meet Bryan.

In the back of Cassidy's mind, too, was the knowledge that her first week in England was drawing to a close. Another week and she would be going home. How could she leave Bryan? Of course they could keep in touch, but she panicked when she thought of the hundreds of miles of land and sea that would separate them.

On Monday evening they went into The Bridge Inn for a drink. It did not really matter now to Cassidy if she was seen, because she was going to make sure that Bryan took her home to Berry House tonight. The time for pretence was over. She was just mulling over how she could explain her deception to him when she saw Leslie walk through the door.

Her first reaction was one of shock and she felt herself shrinking back into a corner. Then she realised this had happened for the best and she stood up, calling out, 'Leslie!'

He hesitated, looking round. He saw her and smiled, coming across, but when he saw Bryan his smile vanished rapidly.

'Enfield,' he said shortly, 'what are you doing here?'

'I'm with my girl, if it's any of your business,' Bryan said equally shortly.

Cassidy looked from one to the other of them, rather worried at their attitudes.

'At least I don't have to introduce you,' she said, trying to smile, but there was a strange, hard look on Bryan's face that disturbed her. Leslie's expression did not bother her at all. She was used to his moods and he was no doubt jealous, but Bryan ... Why did he look like that? As though he would dearly love to knock Leslie down.

'Join us for a drink, Leslie,' Cassidy offered, prepared to be magnanimous. Leslie remained on his feet.

'So this is your "girlfriend," Cassidy,' he sneered.

She blushed. 'I'm sorry about that,' she began, 'but you see...'

Bryan broke in, grabbing hold of her arm, gripping so hard that he hurt her. 'How do you know Leslie Hawthorn?' he demanded.

'He's my cousin. Well, my half-cousin. Bryan, you're hurting me.'

He did not release her. 'Then you're Matthew Hawthorn's granddaughter?'

'Yes.' Cassidy nodded miserably. Why was Bryan looking at her as though he hated her, as though he didn't even know her?

He let go her arm abruptly, almost pushing her away from him.

'But you're not staying at Berry House, Hawthorn's place,' he said.

'Of course she is,' Leslie said. 'Where do you

81

think she's staying?'

'Bryan.' Cassidy tried to touch him, but he pulled away as though her fingers were red hot. 'I—I can explain.'

'Don't bother.' He got to his feet. 'There's nothing to explain. Obviously you thought it better not to tell me who you were. Well, now I know. At least I found out before it was too late.'

He pushed past the table and strode out of the pub. Cassidy stared after him, unable to believe what had just taken place.

At last Leslie sat down. He looked pleased with himself.

'I told you Enfield was a nasty piece of work, didn't I?' He crowed. 'You're a bad girl, Cassidy, lying to me and Grandad, but I'll forgive you.' He slid along the bench seat towards her. 'What a stoke of luck me coming in here tonight. Good riddance, I say.'

Cassidy ignored him; she tried to get to her feet. She must go after Bryan. She must. Had everybody gone crazy? Leslie forced her to sit down again.

'Have a drink, it'll calm your nerves. Forget Enfield. For some unknown reason he appears to have stuck his knife into us Hawthorns. Goodness knows why. He's only a comer-in, but—'

Cassidy could bear it no longer. She moved fast before Leslie could stop her and although he called out to her, she forced her way through the now crowded pub and ran out into the soft darkness outside. She had to go to Bryan. He couldn't do this to her. What was wrong?

She didn't stop running till she got to the house. There was a light on in a room at the front and Cassidy banged on the door with her fist until her hands hurt, screaming out, 'Bryan, let me in! Oh, please let me in.'

Moments passed before the door was opened and Bryan stood there, Amber at his heels. The dog was pleased to see Cassidy, trying to leap up at her. Bryan was not pleased. He caught hold of Amber's collar and yanked her back in a manner Cassidy had never seen him use before.

'Please, Bryan, let me come in,' she begged.

'We've nothing to say to each other.' Bryan held the door only slightly open. The hatred and, more, the hurt, the suspicion were evident on his face.

'How can you say that?' Cassidy demanded, tears of fear and frustration welling into her eyes. 'How could you change so much towards me? Is it because of Leslie? He means nothing to me at all. He's a perfect pest, that's all. Or is it because I didn't tell you who I was? I'd nothing to hide, why should I have, but I didn't want you to come to the house in case Leslie was there. He's got some ridiculous idea about him and me.'

She broke off. Bryan's look was totally implacable.

'Let me in. We can't talk here,' she said.

She was aware that she was humbling herself before him and that her pleas were not moving him one inch, but she couldn't help it. Her world had suddenly become a hideous nightmare and she didn't know why.

Without a word Bryan opened the door wider and Cassidy went inside. The door led directly into the sitting-room. One softly glowing lamp stood in a corner giving the room an intimate, cosy look. Was it only last night that she and Bryan had sat together on the couch, touching one another, kissing, laughing when Amber made herself so obtrusive?

'Won't you at least tell me what it's all about?' Cassidy asked plaintively.

Bryan looked at her coldly. 'First you tell me something. Had you honestly no deeper reason for pretending you were living somewhere else, for not telling me Matthew Hawthorn was your grandfather?'

'Of course I hadn't. I don't know what you mean. Why does it bother you so? I didn't even know you knew my grandfather well enough to hate him, as you so obviously do. I was aware that Leslie knew you on a casual basis and that he didn't like you, but that didn't worry me. Leslie's a pain and totally unlikeable himself.'

'You're way off the mark, Cassidy.' It was the first time he had used her name and, perhaps mistakenly, because he had not softened in the slightest towards her, she saw it

84

as a sign of hope, however faint. 'My relationship with Leslie Hawthorn is far from casual. In fact, it's about on a par with yours.'

Cassidy sat down suddenly, staring up at him. She was unaware that Amber had come to lie across her feet.

'What are you talking about?' she asked him.

'He's my half-cousin, too. Though he doesn't know it. Matthew Hawthorn is my grandfather.'

Cassidy felt stunned. Bryan moved quickly, pouring something from a bottle into a small glass, pressing it into her hand.

'Here, drink this.'

She gulped down the liquid obediently, coughing, gagging as the strange, unfamiliar taste of brandy seared her throat.

She found her tongue at last. 'How can he be? Who are you?'

'I'm Bryan Hawthorn, Esther Hawthorn's illegitimate son.'

It was too much. The words were forcing themselves into her brain, but her brain did not want to accept them. She finished off the brandy and Bryan sat, at last, but made no attempt to touch her or even to move near to her.

As she began to assimilate what Bryan had told her, Cassidy said, 'Esther Hawthorn is my mother's sister. So you're my cousin, not just my half-cousin.'

85

Bryan nodded grimly. 'You're getting there.'

She looked at him and quickly he averted his glance as though he could not, or would not, meet her eyes with his.

'And is that why you're so upset? But, it's hardly my fault, is it? And what difference should it make to our relationship? We were both totally unaware of the other's existence. We're first cousins, but that doesn't matter. Not legally. We can still—'

Bryan leaped up again. 'You're still not getting it are you?' he yelled. 'Aren't you wondering just for a moment what I'm doing here? Isn't it just a little bit too much of a coincidence that Matthew Hawthorn's illegitimate grandson should come to live in Berrybridge? Living under a false surname?' He laughed mirthlessly. 'Enfield! Of course it's the name of a motor-bike. That's why I chose it.'

He sounded full of hatred and bitterness, but surely not against her? She was innocent, coming to Berrybridge on her grandfather's invitation. She had not even known about her Aunt Esther's son until Leslie told her. She still knew none of the details, except what Bryan was telling her now and, oh, how she wished she could cover her ears and shut out his words.

'I came here for the express purpose of getting revenge. My mother was treated abominably. Thrown out by her own father when she needed help most. We're not talking of the Victorian era. This happened less than thirty years ago. That she managed to raise me on her own is all to her credit, but it wasn't easy.'

'Nor for my mother,' Cassidy broke in, determined to have her say, too. 'My mother married but Grandad refused to have anything to do with her. She had to choose between my father and him. Dad died before I was born, so I never knew him, and when Grandad wrote and asked me to come here I didn't want to, but Mam made me see that bitterness and hatred only make things worse. They poison yourself as well as others. I came with an open mind and I'm trying to get to know him. You could, too, if you'd only give him a chance.'

Bryan gave another harsh, joyless laugh. 'There is one big difference, surely you must see that. Matthew Hawthorn knows about you and he *asked* you here. He wants you here. He doesn't know I exist. He's never, not once over the years, tried to make contact with my mother.'

'Did your mother try to contact him?' Cassidy asked quietly.

'Yes. He sent her letters back unopened. In the end it was too much for her. She killed herself when I was fifteen. That was after years of psychiatric treatment. So you see, Cassidy, why I hate that man? I came here, so that some time, some way, I could make him suffer as he

87

made my mother suffer.'

Cassidy said nothing. There did not seem anything she could say. She twisted her hands together.

'I spent some of my childhood with foster parents because my mother was ill, and I lived with them permanently after she died. I don't know why my mother moved to Norfolk, perhaps my father came from there, I just don't know. She never told me anything about my father but she told me plenty about hers. It wasn't a pretty story. When I left school, I got a job in a garage and that's where I began to be interested in motor-bikes. I saved as much as I could and came north.'

When he paused, Cassidy said quickly, 'You've been here three years, you said. Haven't you ever tried to contact the old man during that time?'

'No. I was scared I'd try to kill him.' His voice was steady, without emotion.

'Oh, surely not?' Cassidy cried.

'You don't know how much I hate and detest him. I wanted him to suffer and I couldn't think of a way to make that happen, so I waited. I'd seen him a few times, of course, and I'd met that so-called grandson of his.' He gave another of his short, bitter laughs. 'Leslie Hawthorn didn't seem worth hating, only despising. Then I found I liked living here, especially after I met Rob Marshall and we opened the museum. The local people accepted me and I'll be honest, there were times when I began to forget the real reason I came here, because life was so good.'

Bryan looked at Cassidy for the first time, but his eyes were the eyes of a stranger. 'Then I met you. You were so important to me. I knew I wouldn't have time to think about Matthew Hawthorn. I wanted to get to know you better, then tell you everything. I felt, I believed, you would understand and maybe help me to work through my bitterness, my need for revenge.'

Impulsively, Cassidy put out her hand and touched his arm. 'Oh, Bryan,' she said, 'of course I'll help you. I love you!'

She had said it now. There was no going back. When Bryan snatched his arm away, the rising hope died in Cassidy's heart.

'You're one of them! You're a Hawthorn. You have his blood. So have I but I can't help that. If I married you, I'd be betraying my mother. Every time I looked at you I would remember what he did to her. If we had children, I—' He got up abruptly, unable to finish his sentence.

The thought of being the father of Cassidy's children was poison to him. He did not need to complete his sentence, as she knew by his expression what he had been going to say.

There didn't seem any point in going on. Bryan was far too obsessed. She could see any relationship between them would be a disaster. She got to her feet. If she could just reach the

89

door, leave him, walk away. Her legs felt weak, but she had to keep moving. She must not stop. She must not look back. He neither moved nor called out to her. She opened the door and went out into the warm, dark, silent night. She closed the door behind her and started to walk down the path.

She knew now, beyond any shadow of doubt, that she loved Bryan. She knew her heart was breaking, but she could not rid herself of the image of his hatred. Nothing remained in her mind of the Bryan Enfield she had met and fallen in love with. Bryan Hawthorn was a completely different person and although Cassidy wanted to help him, although she knew his need for revenge had twisted and distorted him, although tears were coursing down her cheeks as she walked because of the dreadful, terrible waste of such a fine and wonderful man, there was nothing she could do about it.

She walked to Berry House. The front door was unlocked but the house seemed to be in darkness except for a light in the hall. Cassidy went slowly up to her room. She had decided she would go home tomorrow. There was no point in staying on. She wanted nothing more to do with her grandfather. She opened the bedroom door and switched on the bedside light. It was then she saw the albums piled on the bed. There were three of them, with old, battered covers.

Automatically, Cassidy went and picked up the first one, leafing slowly through the pages. Someone at some time had lovingly and carefully mounted the family snapshots in the album. Some of the pictures, many of them, were sepia-tinted, decorative, showing men and women, proud looking, unsmiling in old-fashioned, sombre clothing. When Cassidy saw the picture of Elizabeth Cassidy Hawthorn, she recognised her grandmother at once from the picture her mother had at home, a young, sweet-faced person. Seated at her side was a small boy, his hair smartly brushed, his shoes highly polished. Elizabeth carried a very small baby in her arms, wrapped in a white shawl. There was a date on the photograph. It said 1941.

The children must be James and Esther, because Cassidy knew her mother was not born till 1947. James and Esther, both of whom had been tragically lost. James killed whilst still a youth; Esther driven from her home to have her child alone, her father not knowing or caring what had become of her. Now she, too, was dead, by her own hand. Esther, Bryan's mother. Cast aside by Matthew Hawthorn as Cassidy's own mother had been. What a heartless, cruel man he was. How could she possibly align herself with such a person or with Leslie Hawthorn, who himself was self-centred and egotistical?

Cassidy collapsed on to the bed, the open

album in her hands and let the tears run unheeded down her face...

She must have slept. A knocking on the bedroom door awoke her. She was still lying on top of the covers with the photograph albums beside her. She glanced at her watch. It was just before seven and already the morning was sunny and beckoning through the uncurtained windows. Feeling creased, untidy and still tired, Cassidy responded to the persistent knocking on the door.

It was Mrs Dawson. 'Come on down, love,' she urged. 'He wants to see you.'

She looked worried and Cassidy knew who she meant by 'he.' She did not care that she looked a mess; that her hair needed combing and her face washing. What did it matter? She would be leaving later in the day. But first she wanted to see him, wanted to face him. It was time for some plain speaking, old man or no old man.

CHAPTER SEVEN

Cassidy had not bargained for Leslie being there, but he was. Seven o'clock in the morning and he looked as though he had just stepped out of the pages of a men's fashion magazine. Dark blue trousers, pale blue shirt; hair immaculately styled. Only one thing was missing—his smile. He looked peeved, annoyed. He was standing in front of the sitting-room window and he swung round to face Cassidy as she entered.

Matthew Hawthorn occupied his usual chair, a patriarchal figure in a tweed jacket; his rather florid cheeks looking freshly shaved, gnarled hand gripping his walking-stick.

Cassidy, in an attempt at bravado, so they would not know how terrible she felt, spoke first. 'You're here early, Leslie. Did you stay the night?' She knew he hadn't. He wasn't wearing the same clothes, unlike herself. She must look awful.

It was her grandfather who answered, sharply, in a voice that sent a chill down Cassidy's spine. 'No, he didn't. He was here at the crack of dawn, practically dragging me out of bed. Telling me some wild story about a chap you've been seeing. The one that runs the bike museum. Is it true?'

'I saw them together, Grandad,' Leslie put in sneeringly.

'Shut your mouth. I'm not talking to you,' Matthew snapped.

Leslie sank on to a chair like a whipped puppy. He didn't say anything else.

Matthew turned to Cassidy. 'Well?' Just the one word.

She stood her ground, lifting her head defiantly. 'Yes.' She, too, spoke only one word.

'I never had you marked down as a liar, lass.'

The old man's voice was almost sad.

'I'm not. Well, not usually, but I thought you'd be angry and I was right, you are. So I was justified in not telling you the truth, wasn't I?'

'Going behind my back. Sneaking in and out of the house. For goodness' sake, Cassidy, what do you see in a fellow like Enfield?'

She nearly blurted out, 'Hawthorn,' and only just managed to stop herself. Oh, she intended saying it, but she wasn't going to say anything in front of Leslie.

He had been chastened by her grandfather and Cassidy could see he was seething inwardly, but there was no way she was going to discuss Bryan or his mother whilst Leslie Hawthorn was around. If necessary, she would ask him to leave. What had induced him in the first place, to come to the house at this ungodly hour, rousing them up, tittle-tattling? How despicable he was! And what good did he think it would do him? Did he think he only had to whine at the old man to be able to get his own way?

She could see her grandfather expected some response to his question.

'I like Bryan,' she said. 'Please don't talk about him as though he's dirt in the road.'

'Has he made a pass at you?'

The quaintness of the expression did not prevent Cassidy from blushing furiously. She could tell by the look on Matthew's face that he took the blushing to indicate guilt.

'No, he hasn't,' she cried, 'but even if he had it wouldn't be any of your business. I'm over twenty-one.'

The walking-stick thudded angrily on the floor. It seemed to be one of his favourite gestures.

'I've told you before and I'll tell you again, whilst you're under my roof you're my responsibility. I don't care whether you're twenty-one or forty-one, you'll keep a civil tongue in your head when you address me, young lady!'

She was afraid of him, but by the blessed St Joseph she was not going to let him see it, because she was also very angry now and she knew she had nothing to lose by answering back. She had lost Bryan. She did not care about anyone or anything else.

'I'm not my mother, Grandad,' she flung at him, 'and I'm not my Aunt Esther either, so don't you be after thinking you can threaten and browbeat me. I didn't want to come here in the first place and I only agreed to please Mam, but I'm not staying, no, not if you beg me to on your bended knees. I'm leaving today.'

Leslie was galvanised into action at her words, leaping up as though someone had stuck a pin in him.

'You can't leave!' he screeched, his face going a horrible, mottled red. 'Tell her you want her to marry me. She hasn't given me a

95

chance. All she does is put me down and then goes after Enfield. Tell her about the money and the house. I won't give up what's rightfully mine, just because she won't marry me. I won't just stand by and see her take it all.'

The walking-stick lashed out, striking Leslie across the arm. He yelped in pain, but it stemmed the torrent of words in an instant.

'Sit down, lad, you've said more than enough.'

'But, Grandad—' he protested.

The old man half-rose out of his chair, brandishing the stick like a sword.

'Do you want me to batter you round the head, boy?'

He would do himself harm if he didn't calm down, Cassidy thought. Leslie sat again, rubbing his arm. Cassidy heard him muttering under his breath. Lucky for him Matthew did not seem to do so.

The words Leslie had spoken were going round and round in her head. His meaning was obvious. Her grandfather intended to leave her everything. Leslie would only get his share if they married. How typical of this cruel, hard, old man to make such a stipulation. Who did he think he was, manipulating people's lives? He must have gone over the matter with Leslie prior to her arrival and naturally, someone like Leslie, a man who liked power and wealth, would readily agree. But why would her grandfather want them to marry?

96

Matthew Hawthorn looked at her. It seemed as though all his anger had suddenly drained away. He looked sad; if she had not known better, Cassidy would even say frightened. His voice was low when he asked. 'How do you know about your Aunt Esther, girl?'

Cassidy hesitated. She could say her mother had told her, but that was not strictly true. She could come straight out now and tell what she knew about Bryan but that would mean getting rid of Leslie first. Or she could say it was Leslie himself who had told her about Esther. She glanced at Leslie. He looked terrified. Cassidy's brow creased in perplexity till she realised what he was scared of. He didn't want the old man to know he had talked about Esther to Cassidy. Leslie must be thinking Cassidy was going to mention his name. She saw her opportunity to get rid of him. Quickly she said, 'Grandad, I've got to speak to you privately, about Bryan. It's got nothing to do with Leslie. I'm not trying to evade your question, but I can't speak in front of Leslie.'

Her cousin was on his feet in an instant.

'I've got to go anyway, Grandad,' he said with a false and irritating brightness.

Matthew turned his sombre gaze upon the young man.

'I know you're worried about your inheritance,' the old man said, sarcasm in his voice. 'But there's no need.'

'I'll come tonight, shall I?' Leslie looked up.

He was almost cringing, ready to lick the old man's boots. Cassidy's dislike for him increased.

'Suit yourself.'

'Right. See you. And you, Cassidy.'

Then she and her grandfather were alone.

'Now, lass, there's just you and me,' Matthew said, trying, she was sure, to inject kindness, patience into his voice.

That would soon go when he heard what she had to say!

'Yes.' Cassidy was not sure she wanted to tell him anything now.

'Who told you about Esther? And what exactly do you know about her?'

'I've always known Mam had a brother and sister. I know James died but I didn't know my Aunt Esther committed suicide.' As soon as the words were spoken, Cassidy regretted them. It was too soon; too abrupt. Of course her grandfather did not know Esther was dead. Her mother had not known either. Very little had been said about either James or Esther. Certainly Cassidy had never been told about Esther's baby.

She watched now as the colour left the old man's face; as he gripped the arms of his chair and let his walking-stick thud on to the carpet.

'Esther ... dead?' His voice was strangled, his old, and now Cassidy saw, tired-looking eyes staring at her in total disbelief.

98

'Grandad.' Impulsively, Cassidy went and kneeled by his chair, catching hold of one of his broad, gnarled hands. It was so cold. 'I'm sorry. It was Bryan who told me.'

Some spark of his previous anger returned. 'Enfield?'

Cassidy nodded. 'Yes. Except his name isn't Enfield. It's Hawthorn. He's Esther's son.' There was no point in holding back now. She couldn't shock him any deeper. She had to proceed, to be cruel to be kind. Anyway, didn't she want him to know the truth? He had hurt so many people in the past. Now it was his turn.

She told him all that Bryan had told her. She recounted their meeting with Leslie in the pub and how it had all come out. When she finished she saw that Matthew was crying, silent tears spilling down his cheeks. Compassion began to swell in her, till, as though suddenly becoming aware of the wetness in his eyes, the old man rubbed at them fiercely, taking a clean white handkerchief from his pocket and wiping his cheeks.

'So Esther's kid came here, did he?' he growled, withdrawing his hand from under Cassidy's own in a rough, jerking movement. 'Biding his time. Hoping to catch me unawares. What did he intend to do? Have you any idea, lass? Come gunning for me, perhaps? Maybe set fire to the house with me in it. He could hardly hope to ruin me financially.'

He was recovering rapidly and Cassidy

could see he was enjoying it. Perhaps he was attempting to hide his true feelings. Perhaps he desperately wanted to appear unmoved, hard, tough in front of her. She knew the news of Esther's death had hurt him, but his sorrow had been brief, and as it faded, so did the compassion she felt for him. She got to her feet.

'I love Bryan, Grandad,' she said. 'But he hates me as much as he hates you. He thinks I tried to hide from him that I was your granddaughter. He won't listen to anything I say. He doesn't want to see me any more—'

She broke off as Matthew struggled awkwardly to his feet, waving his hand impatiently towards his stick, which mechanically Cassidy retrieved and handed to him.

'Good, good, I'm glad to hear it.' The strength, the power, the ... arrogance were all back there in his voice. 'He could never be a Hawthorn. Oh, he may bear the name, but he's not entitled to it. He doesn't scare me. It would take more than a madman on a motor-bike to scare Matthew Hawthorn. Cassidy, lass, he's not worth weeping over. I've got plans for you. For you and Leslie.' His eyes twinkled but there was an irrational glint there, too, that frightened Cassidy, and seemed to hold her mute before him like a rabbit caught in a car's headlights, on a dark, country road.

'Perhaps I wasn't going to tell you just yet, but happen it's for the best that Leslie's spoken out. Don't be put off by his manner. He's a good lad. He's going places. He's good at making brass as well. Give him a chance. You'll make an old man very happy. And if you and Leslie get hitched, I'll see you want for nothing, either of you. Give me a great grandson before I go, let's get the Hawthorn name back on the road.'

His voice rose triumphantly and Cassidy backed away from him in horror. Was he insane? He was certainly drunk with ambition and hope. He had dismissed his daughter Esther from his mind after shedding only a few brief, meaningless tears over her. He had not spared even that much for his grandson, Bryan. He was not in the least curious about Bryan who was his own flesh and blood just as she was; just as Leslie was. What sort of a man was he?

'Nay, lass, don't look so scared. We'll say no more about you and Enfield.' He wasn't even going to acknowledge that Bryan bore his name. Matthew reached out a hand towards her.

'Keep away from me!' Cassidy cried. 'I don't want you or your money and I wouldn't marry Leslie if he was the last man on earth. I'm leaving here, Grandad. I'm going back to Ireland. Today. I never want to see you again.'

The proffered hand dropped to the old man's side; the placatory smile vanished.

'What on earth are you talking about?' he

101

thundered.

'I hate you. I despise you for what you've done to Bryan and for what you did to my mother.' Cassidy was beside herself now, tears coursing down her cheeks. 'You're a monster with no heart and I hope I never see you again!'

She turned on those words and ran from the room, from the house, down the drive and out on to the road. She saw the church with its over-crowded, neglected churchyard and without looking ran across the road and inside the gates. Without stopping she ran up the walk to the church door, but when she tried the door it was locked. Foolishly, she banged her fists against the stout wood of the door. It wasn't a Catholic church, but, oh, how she wanted, how she needed to find sanctuary there. All too soon she realised no-one was going to open the door for her and she stood with her head buried in her hands, crying softly.

When she felt hands on her shoulders, she stiffened in fear, but the hands were gentle, the voice, speaking behind her, quiet and kind.

'Cassidy, darling, don't cry.' Bryan swung her round and enveloped her in his arms. 'I'm sorry. I'm so sorry. It isn't your fault and I love you so much!'

Cassidy wept more tears but now they were tears of joy.

Bryan made her some tea and toast and Cassidy sat with Amber stretched out at her feet whilst she ate and drank. Food had never tasted so good. With the words Bryan had spoken and the way he had held her, Cassidy's misery, pain and depression had lifted like a cloak from her shoulders.

Bryan had brought her to his house, talking to her all the time, telling her he loved her, telling her his plans. Plans that she would be a part of. He did not need to ask her if she would go along with him. He knew she would, as she herself instinctively knew that their love for one another would endure for ever and that one day, soon, they would get married.

First they were going to Norfolk. Bryan had said, 'I want to go home and Swaffham is my home. We can stay with my foster mother. It's a bit short notice, but she'll understand. I'll phone her first, let her know we're coming. You'll like her, Cassidy. I know you will.'

Cassidy looked at him. 'So soon?' she said.

He nodded. 'I need to get away from here, Cassidy. I need breathing space. After you'd left I did a great deal of thinking and I realised you were right. I was consumed with hatred and anger, and it was eating me away, poisoning me. Because of how I felt about Matthew Hawthorn, I thought I had lost the only person next to my mother that I've ever really loved. I asked myself if my need for revenge was stronger than my love for you, and of course, it wasn't.' He took hold of her hand. 'I need you with me, love. This obsession has been with me a long time and I can't rid myself of it alone. I need you to help me. Last night you said you would.'

'And I will,' Cassidy broke in, squeezing his fingers.

'So come with me to Norfolk. I won't stay there, because my work is here, but just for a while. After what you've just told me about you and your grandfather, it seems to me you need breathing space, too.'

It was true; she did. She had intended going back to Ireland but only because she thought she had lost Bryan. Now she would have another week before her official holiday here was over. Then would be soon enough to let her mother know what was happening. By that time she and Bryan would have made plans for their future.

There were some things, perhaps, that Cassidy did not want to see and know about, but if she intended to share Bryan's life, she had to know everything she could about him and he about her. There must be nothing hidden, no more secrets.

'I—I don't want to go back to the house,' she confessed, the very thought of having to face her grandfather again making her shake.

'You don't have to,' Bryan assured her. 'I'll buy you everything you need. I can lend you a jacket and some jeans to travel in. They'll bury you, but no matter.'

'Are we going on the bike?'

104

Bryan grinned and Cassidy melted when she saw the tension and strain vanish from his face. 'Of course.'

'What about Amber?' she asked, stroking the dog's silky fur.

'Rob's looking after her. My partner.'

Cassidy nodded. 'He ... he might worry about me,' she murmured, a small feeling of guilt making her hesitate. Her grandfather might be harsh and cruel, but he was an old man—what if something should happen to him? Could she simply leave Berrybridge without telling him? Could she leave all her possessions in the house?

'Let him worry. It will do him good,' Bryan said. Seeing her uncertainty, he put his arm around her shoulders and squeezed. 'It's for the best, love, believe me. If you go back, and you've just said you don't want to, he'll try to persuade you to stay. He'll put pressure on you. Do you want all that?'

No, she didn't. She made up her mind. 'All right, but let's leave today,' she said, 'then I won't have time to change my mind.'

'Suits me,' Bryan said. 'I was hoping you'd say that.'

CHAPTER EIGHT

Cassidy had imagined that even on a flying machine like Bryan's bike it would have taken much longer to get to Norfolk but they arrived in the early afternoon and had stopped off for lunch on the way at the small Lincolnshire town of Sleaford. They had travelled via motorways and A-roads through ever varying scenery. Cassidy considered herself a seasoned motor-bike pillion rider by now and had enjoyed every minute of the journey.

Sleaford was pretty, with a busy main street, a river, crossed by tiny bridges, where swans were nesting; a square with a tourist information centre housed in a converted windmill, and various restaurants and tea rooms tucked away out of sight in back streets and yards.

After they had had something to eat, Bryan pressed some money into Cassidy's hand and told her to buy what she needed in the way of clothes, toiletries etc. She took the money reluctantly saying, 'Well, only as a loan till I get my own money back.'

Bryan shrugged carelessly. 'Fair enough,' he said. 'It'll be nice to have a wife who prefers to spend her own money.'

Cassidy's face grew hot. 'Is that a proposal?' she asked quietly.

He looked deep into her eyes. 'Sounds very much like one to me,' he said.

They kissed then and Cassidy knew it was the happiest moment of her life.

The bike flew along the roads towards Swaffham and Cassidy's heart flew with it. It was only when they finally reached Bryan's home that she remembered why they were here and sadness overtook her again.

She did not let Bryan see how she felt. He was so intent on pointing out places of interest, so keen to see the old, familiar buildings of the quaint Norfolk market town; the school he had attended, the garage where he had his first job after leaving school, that Cassidy was sure he was not thinking about Matthew Hawthorn at all. Cassidy did not want to think about him either, but found it impossible to forget completely.

Bryan's house was on a small, narrow street leading directly from the market square. A row of neat, terraced houses with well-tended gardens, running at right angles to a playing field with goal posts and wide, green lawns.

As Bryan turned the bike into the street's narrow opening, Cassidy saw the name of it on the wall of the corner building. 'The Pightle.'

'What does it mean?' Cassidy asked as they removed their helmets.

'It's an old Suffolk word actually,' Bryan told her, 'meaning a small meadow.' He smiled and waved his arm in the direction of the playing fields. 'Well, there's your meadow … sort of,' he said.

The house was as neat as a new pin. His foster mother, Auntie Annie, was away visiting friends. In the small kitchen a note was propped on the worktop, welcoming Bryan back, saying that the fridge was well stocked and that there was fresh bread in the bin. Bryan leaned against the cupboards.

'Good old Auntie Annie. One of the best,' he said.

Then they were in each other's arms, kissing, and Cassidy did not want their kiss to end.

'I love you so much,' Bryan whispered. 'I want us to get married as soon as we can. I know we haven't known one another very long, but I'm sure of my feelings. Are you?'

Cassidy nodded eagerly. 'Quite sure. Would you be prepared to marry me in a Catholic church, Bryan?'

He held her away from him. 'Let's say I'd be prepared to have your church's blessing, but I was thinking of something quick. A registry office ceremony as soon as residency legalities are established.'

He must have noticed her hesitancy, her slight discomfiture but he said nothing. A quickie wedding was not what Cassidy had dreamed of. What girl did? She had wanted a white dress, bridesmaids and a choir. She had wanted her mother to be present. But then she had envisaged marrying an Irish boy in their

108

local church with a beaming Father MacIlvenny conducting the service.

Well, she wasn't in love with an Irish boy, and she wasn't even in Ireland. Bryan was right. They would have a civil ceremony and later the Church's blessing, if not its approval. Bryan was not a Catholic and she would not press him to change his religion. When they eventually went back to Berrybridge, and she knew they would have to, it would be as man and wife, presenting both her grandfather and the Church with a fait accompli. A situation which she would not dwell on and therefore would not worry about.

In the meantime, she was eager to explore this neat little house. Where would she sleep tonight? When would she meet Auntie Annie? She was filled with an anticipatory thrill when these questions posed themselves.

'A cup of tea first, I think.' She smiled happily at Bryan. 'Then you can give me a conducted tour.'

He readily agreed to that. Apparently they would have to be resident in Swaffham for only seven days before being able to make application to marry. It would mean, in fact, a trip into Norwich to the register office but neither of them would mind that. Bryan told her it was an interesting city and that was enough for her to want to go there. Three weeks after making the application, their wedding could take place.

Bryan wanted to ask Auntie Annie to be a witness for their wedding and, of course, she readily agreed.

Cassidy liked her on sight. She was small, rounded, warm and homely, probably now in her late sixties. She had wept happy tears when she came home to find Bryan rushing round to make tea and produce home-made cake. She kissed Cassidy and talked all the time, mostly about Bryan, though he pretended to be horrified at certain revelations of his childhood.

It was only when she was alone for a while with Cassidy when Bryan had gone into the town to pick up some shopping for her, that Auntie Annie became serious and afterwards, Cassidy did wonder if Bryan had gone out of the way deliberately to allow them time to get to know one another, and to talk. Perhaps there were things he wanted Cassidy to know but felt unable to mention them himself.

'Let's have another cup of tea, shall we?' Auntie Annie suggested, re-filling the kettle.

The kitchen was pleasant and sunny with looped net curtains at the diamond-paned windows. A small, round table stood in the middle of the room with a bowl of pansies, picked, Cassidy was sure, from Auntie Annie's own small, well-kept garden.

As they sat to drink their tea, Auntie Annie said, 'He's a grand lad. Malcolm and I never had any children of our own, but Bryan made

110

up for all that. Especially after his mother died and he came to live with us permanently.'

Cassidy smiled. 'I'm sure you did your best to make him happy,' she said.

The older woman nodded. 'We did, but sometimes it wasn't easy. He was very upset about his mother, of course. I presume you know all about her.'

'Yes. You see, Bryan didn't mention it, but he and I are cousins.' And Cassidy told Auntie Annie the whole story, her own story as well as Bryan's. The words flowed easily from her because Bryan's foster mother was a good, patient listener. When Cassidy had finished her story, Auntie Annie put her hand on top of Cassidy's own, patting it gently.

'You're very lucky to have found one another,' she said, 'and would you ever have met if it hadn't been for your troubles? Sometimes good comes from bad, doesn't it? I know you'll both be very happy.'

No wonder Bryan thought the world of this woman. The contrast between her and Matthew Hawthorn didn't bear thinking about and Auntie Annie was not of their flesh and blood as Matthew was.

'Did—did you know Bryan's mother?' Cassidy asked tentatively.

'We met her once or twice but we didn't know her well. She was a very disturbed woman, and so young, or so it seemed to us. Frail, you might say. The doctors did their best

111

for her but it was as though—oh, how can I describe it? As though she had a great weight and worry on her shoulders all the time.

'Bryan was a lovely child. He was about eight, I should say, when first he came to us. His mother had done a wonderful job with him in some ways. He was polite, friendly, intelligent, but nervous, too, you know, and constantly asking if his mother would be all right. This went on for a few years and each time Esther had a spell in hospital, Bryan came to us. I always tried to comfort him and to be optimistic about his mother so when she died, it seemed all the more of a shock to him. I'm afraid he was very bitter towards his grandfather.'

'Yes, I know.' Cassidy's voice was sad.

'He blamed his mother's precarious state of health and her death on his grandfather,' Auntie Annie said. 'I tried to tell him not to hate, but well—' She smiled wistfully. 'You know how he was. You've just told me what he was doing in Berrybridge.' Her face brightened. 'Anyway, that's all in the past now. It's the future that counts and you and Bryan have a wonderful future ahead of you. Where will you live? Have you decided?'

'In Berrybridge, I expect,' Cassidy said. 'That's where Bryan's work is and he lives for that museum. I can't see him giving it up. We'll have to see.'

Personally, Cassidy had her doubts about

the wisdom of setting up home so near her grandfather, unless, of course, the impossible happened, a miracle occurred and she and Bryan were reconciled to the old man. Only time would tell if that would come about. Right now, it did not seem very likely. Thoughts flashed through Cassidy's mind about how Matthew would be reacting to her disappearance. She could not, despite her happiness at being with Bryan, rid herself of vague feelings of guilt.

She became aware that Auntie Annie was speaking to her again.

'There is a box upstairs that belonged to Bryan's mother. It's a sort of small metal trunk affair. I've no idea what's in it but Esther left it here once, for safe-keeping, she said. After she died I did ask Bryan if he wanted it and I told him where the key was, but as far as I know he's never even looked inside. I think he was afraid he'd be too upset sorting through his mother's possessions, but I'm wondering now, dear, whether it's the right time to mention it again. What do you think?'

'I don't know,' Cassidy admitted. 'Would you like me to mention it to Bryan?'

'If you wouldn't mind. Of course, it can stay where it is without any trouble to anybody if that's what Bryan wants.'

Cassidy's naturally curious nature hoped that Bryan would want to take the box and look through its contents.

113

At first, to Cassidy's dismay, Bryan stubbornly refused to have anything to do with his mother's belongings. What's more, he didn't want her to look at them either and got quite cross at the very mention of the tin trunk. Cassidy decided to bide her time. If Bryan said 'No' there was very little she could do about it.

She was disappointed because she had a strong feeling that somewhere in that box would be some clues as to what sort of a person Esther Hawthorn really was, and what really lay behind her illness and her suicide. Bryan was convinced it was the way her father had treated her. Quite possibly he was right, but Cassidy had niggling doubts that there could be more.

Bryan was in a subdued mood for the rest of the evening. Cassidy believed it was because he'd been reminded of the box. For this one reason alone, it would be much better for him to go through the box's contents. Only how was she going to be able to put this across to him?

'About my mother's box. You can take a look through it, if you like.' Cassidy jumped up and put her arms round Bryan's neck, kissing him on the mouth.

'Hey, steady on!' he cried.

Cassidy laughed. 'Sorry and thanks.'

Bryan gave her a sideways glance. 'What for? You only want to look through the box because you're a nosy old biddy.'

'Partly,' she admitted. 'Aren't you just a teeny weeny bit curious yourself?'

Bryan shook his head. 'No, and I don't want to take a trip down memory lane with you. Is that clear?'

'Surely you'll want to know—' Cassidy began but Bryan silenced her by grabbing hold of her and planting another kiss on her mouth.

'I don't want to know anything,' he told her and continued to kiss her.

They both forgot about the box for quite some time.

*   *   *

Cassidy got her opportunity to look through the box next afternoon. It was not very large, about the size of a small suitcase, made of black, painted metal with a slightly domed lid. It was a battered and well-used trunk, and the very sight and feel of it induced nostalgic dreams in Cassidy.

How many owners had the box had? How many different possessions, perhaps treasured and loved, had it contained? What did it contain now?

There was a key on a piece of string hanging from the leather handle on the side. Bryan told Cassidy he was going over to a place called Aylsham that afternoon to look at some bikes. What else? Cassidy thought happily, waving him off, knowing she had all the afternoon to herself to browse through the contents of Esther's trunk.

And yet, despite her eagerness, it was with some trepidation that she unlocked the lock and gently opened the hinged lid. On top lay folded sheets of tissue paper, yellowing now, fragile, which Cassidy laid carefully on one side. Next there were some clothes. Women's clothes, some jumpers and old-fashioned skirts. A couple of floral cotton dresses. Cassidy held up one or two of the items. If they had belonged to Bryan's mother, she must have been very tall and slim.

Beneath the women's clothes was another layer of tissue paper and under that a collection of neatly-folded baby clothes—matinee coats, bootees, bonnets, two embroidered nightgowns, small cream-coloured baby vests of the old-fashioned, wrapover type.

Cassidy picked up a small, white jacket and held it against her cheek. It felt soft. They must be Bryan's baby clothes, lovingly stored away by his mother. How tiny they were! It was difficult to imagine the tall, handsome man she loved so much as a small baby. Her interest thoroughly roused now, Cassidy went on to the next layer.

There seemed to be a pile of old newspaper cuttings. She was about to look through them when she saw the envelopes fastened together with white tape. There must have been about a dozen in all, addressed in a heavy, flamboyant

116

handwriting. The addressee was Miss Esther Hawthorn at, of all places, a Leeds address. None of the envelopes had been opened. Who could they be from? When had Esther ever lived in Leeds?

Cassidy hesitated. The letters were not hers. Perhaps Bryan should be the one to open them, now. And yet, would he do so? Wasn't he more likely to insist they remained sealed and unread? Before she could change her mind, Cassidy slit open the first envelope in the pile and unfolded the sheets of thin white paper.

She read the sender's address and her heart lurched. It was her grandfather's house and the date was in January 1962, the year in which Cassidy knew Bryan had been born. Her eyes went to the signature at the bottom of the letter. *All my love, Dad.*

With thumping heart she read the letter which began, *My dearest Esther.* The contents of the letter were plain and went totally against what Bryan had told her. Far from Esther's letters to Matthew Hawthorn being ignored and returned unopened, she had refused to answer *his* letters. This one pleaded for some word of her, some news about the baby. Matthew begged his daughter's forgiveness and asked Esther to come home and bring the child with her.

However, Matthew was quite adamant that he would not seek Esther out if she did not want him to. The letter referred to someone

117

called Laura Martin, whoever she might be, who had given Matthew his daughter's address. Cassidy sat a long time holding the letter in her hand. She would have to read the others. Scanning through them, she saw they were all to the same address and when she did open the envelopes she discovered they were all written within the space of about a month, all pleading with Esther to go home.

Cassidy felt shocked; numb. For the first time she experienced a deep stirring of sympathy for her grandfather. Surely this discovery put an entirely different complexion on the situation. Surely even Bryan must see this. But would he? Would he even listen to her? She would make him listen. He had to know the truth.

Carefully she re-fastened the tape around the letters. Now she would look at the old newspaper cuttings. She picked them up and a further envelope fluttered out of the pages. This one was a long, narrow, buff-coloured envelope, official-looking and devoid of any name or address. It was not sealed and Cassidy took out the contents. Two folded documents. The first was Bryan's birth certificate which left a blank where the father's name should be, and gave Esther's address as the same Leeds one to where Matthew's letters had been sent.

The other document was a death certificate and when Cassidy read it, the document dropped from her suddenly-lifeless fingers on to the table in front of her. No, it couldn't be true! There must be some mistake. It was the death certificate of a male child. A three-month-old baby who had died of bronchial pneumonia in a Leeds hospital. The baby's name was Bryan Hawthorn.

Cassidy felt as though she was going to pass out. Her head felt light, empty. She half-rose from her chair, meaning to fetch herself a glass of water, but her legs were shaking so much she had to sit down again. She picked up the death certificate and studied it closely, letting the details penetrate her stunned mind. If Bryan Hawthorn had died at the age of three months, who was the man she loved? There were only the newspaper cuttings left unread, and Cassidy had a dreadful, frightened premonition that in them would lie the answer to her unspoken question.

She picked them up and opened them out. She only needed to read the stark black headlines to know the truth at once, and also to know the obvious reason why Esther Hawthorn, after years of torment had eventually been driven to suicide.

No Clues In Midland Baby Snatch. Where Is The Thompson Baby?

CHAPTER NINE

There was only one way. Cassidy laid the newspapers, the letters and the certificates out flat in Bryan's room where he could not possibly avoid them. If she had tried to explain to him she knew words would have failed her, or worse, Bryan would have refused to listen to her.

When he came back later in the afternoon she greeted him warmly, but before he went to change in the room where the awful truth was waiting to confront him, Cassidy took herself off to the bathroom, saying she was going to have a bath. It was cowardly of her and she half expected Bryan to ask her why, after she had had all afternoon to herself, was she disappearing as soon as he got back. She noticed that he made no mention of the box and this seemed to make what she had done worse, but there was no going back.

She hurried in, locking the bathroom door, running both taps at full, lingering a long time in the bath, drying herself with exaggerated slowness when she got out. All the while the house seemed to be silent, unmoving around her.

She went into Bryan's room. Bryan was sitting on the bed, a mug of cold, untouched coffee by him. The newspaper cuttings, the certificates were now in a neatly-folded pile. Cassidy's heart sank. Hadn't he looked at them? Was she going to have to explain after all? Bryan looked up and it was enough. His eyes stared at her blankly. His skin was pale.

'Bryan,' she whispered, moving towards the table.

'Oh, Cassidy, what a mess!' he said, and then to her horror he burst into tears. She put her arms round him and held him tightly, saying she was sorry, saying she had handled it all wrong, that she should have broken it to him gently.

Bryan shook his head vigorously. 'No, it was better this way.' His voice was choking and he rubbed his hand across his eyes.

Cassidy sat by him holding his hand.

Bryan went on. 'I wouldn't have listened to you,' he said, confirming what she already knew.

'Oh, Cassidy, I never knew. And all these years, since my mother died, the truth about her, about me, has been locked away in that damned box.' He smiled a watery smile. 'I'm just grateful I didn't look before I met you, Cassidy. I don't know what I should do now if I didn't have you.'

'Darling,' Cassidy murmured.

She said nothing else because she could sense Bryan wanted to talk. Let him spill it all out. She would listen for as long as she had to.

'So, it wasn't the old man's fault after all. I

121

spent all those years hating him, feeding off my own hatred and all for nothing. And I'm not even his grandson. Hey, Cassidy, do you realise, we're not really cousins?'

His voice was bright, too bright, with a harsh, brittle quality as though he could easily break down and cry again.

'What on earth was my mother doing in the Midlands, anyway? Wandering about like a gipsy, by the look of it. She must have had no friends, nobody at all.'

'There was Laura Martin,' Cassidy broke in. 'She gave Grandfather Esther's address.'

Bryan nodded. 'Yes. I wonder why she did that and who she was? Well, I don't suppose we shall ever know. There's a lot we shall never know. Who I am, for instance. Poor people, having their baby snatched. What was she thinking of? How could she do a thing like that?'

It had happened a long time ago but it was as real to Bryan now, to both of them, as though it had only happened yesterday. Cassidy did not want Bryan to blame his mother. She did not want the festering hatred to be transferred from Matthew to Esther.

She said, 'Your mother lost her baby and that must have been terrible for her. I expect she left Leeds in an attempt to make a new start. We can only guess at how she felt and what she did, but I'm sure it must be a devastating experience to go through all that

Esther must have gone through, and then lose your child. We—we must try to understand, if we can.'

'I know.' Bryan's voice was sad. 'I still love her. She was good to me and now I know what drove her to that form of madness.' Suddenly he thumped his hand on the table. 'Why on earth didn't she go back home? Your grandfather wanted her. She would have been safe there, especially after the baby died. I can't understand why my mother should want me to think she had written to Matthew only to have her letters returned.'

'She was a woman in torment,' Cassidy said. 'And Grandfather did send her away in the beginning.'

'That's true. But I don't hate him. My hatred for him has never been the same since meeting you, Cassidy, and now, of course, I know there was no need for it in the first place.' He sighed. 'What a waste!'

'Do we keep all this to ourselves, Bryan?' Cassidy asked.

He looked at her. He put his hand against her cheek. 'What else can we do? The Thompsons, whoever they are, will have lived their lives without their son, without me, that is. I can hardly turn up on their doorstep out of the blue, can I? That would be even more cruel than what Esther did. And she'll always be my mother. I can never think of her as anything else.'

123

Cassidy agreed with Bryan, but deep inside was a feeling that if she were poor Mrs Thompson, she would welcome news of her lost child, however much time had gone by. A mother would never forget her baby; just as Esther had never forgotten hers and had been driven to take someone else's when he died. Cassidy was sure the Thompsons, in late middle-age now, even if they had had other children, would always be aware of an empty, desolate ache for the one who was lost. It was in Bryan's power to assuage that ache. He only had to pick up the phone and call the newspaper from which the cuttings came and the whole affair would be set in motion again. But now was the wrong time. It was better to wait and give themselves time to accept the truth.

There was one thing they could do, though, and surely Bryan would agree. They could go back to Berrybridge and make their peace with Matthew. As far as he was concerned, Bryan was Esther's son. Cassidy remembered how her grandfather had reacted to the news of Esther's death. True, he had quickly recovered himself, but not before he had broken down and wept before her. No, in the light of Matthew's poignant letters, his attempts to become reconciled with his daughter, Cassidy felt it was up to her and Bryan to make the first move.

She heard Bryan saying, 'What are you

thinking about, love?' and haltingly, she told him what was in her mind.

He looked away from her. 'I don't know if I'm ready for that,' he said. 'I don't know if I can carry it off—pretending to be his grandson, I mean.'

'But you are, Bryan. You're as much Matthew Hawthorn's grandson as though you were Esther's legally-adopted son.'

Bryan smiled wanly. 'You're kidding yourself, Cassidy,' he told her. 'It isn't the same thing at all and even if it was, wouldn't we be deceiving the old man? Can we do that? There's no love lost between us. Has all this changed anything?'

'We must make it change things,' Cassidy said fervently. 'We know now how Grandfather felt about Esther. He was hurt, too, and guilty, and no doubt full of remorse. Isn't it time to bury the past completely? And I'm not just thinking about you and Esther. There's me, too, and Mam. I want it to end. At least, I want to give it a try.'

Wasn't it odd that she should feel so strongly about it when only a few short days ago, she had run away from her grandfather's house? Well, she was ready to return now.

'And what about us?' Bryan said. 'Do we go back as man and wife, or do we wait?'

She hesitated. She wanted to marry Bryan more than anything in the world, but she was suddenly having visions of a reconciliation

125

with her grandfather, of him and Bryan shaking hands. Perhaps she was a fool, but she was willing to take a chance.

'Let's wait,' she said. 'Let's get married in church.'

* * *

They agreed they wouldn't discuss the matter any further but it wasn't easy. Cassidy was constantly aware that Bryan was rather quiet and subdued. He kept making a conscious effort to snap out of his morose moods but it wasn't easy for him. The trunk was packed, locked and stashed away on top of a wardrobe. It should have been out of sight, out of mind, but of course, it wasn't.

Later in the day, Cassidy had a longing to find out how her mother was. She decided to ring Mrs Mulligan but would not say where she was or ask her mother to phone her back as she generally did, but merely enquire as to her well-being.

They intended returning to Yorkshire in a couple of days, so Cassidy was able to pacify her troubled conscience in this respect. Bryan had said, 'Don't go thinking the old man will welcome us with open arms. We know he has a soft heart under that crusty exterior, but we can't very well tell him how we know, can we?'

Cassidy agreed that they couldn't. She would cross that bridge when she came to it.

She phoned just after six o'clock. It always amazed her how quickly she could get through to the post office and how clear Mrs Mulligan's voice was.

'Hello, Mrs Mulligan?' she said. 'It's me, Cassidy. Do you think you could pass a message on to Mam for me, please?'

Mrs Mulligan's cheerful, loud voice came over the phone.

'Sure, and I'd be glad to, Cassidy, except your mam's not at home, but surely you must know that, for hasn't she gone to England to see you?'

'To see me? But, why?' Her mother in England? In Berrybridge? Fear fluttered in Cassidy.

'Because of your grandfather, of course. What's the matter with you, girl? You're after living in the same house as the old man and you don't know he's taken a bad turn.'

Cassidy's heart was thumping now.

'What sort of turn?'

'A stroke, so I'm told. Didn't I take the message meself only the other day? And your mother phoning back and leaving right away. Are you not there, Cassidy? You don't seem to know what's going on, so you don't.'

'No, no, I'm not in Berrybridge,' Cassidy finally admitted. 'Do you know how badly my grandfather is, Mrs Mulligan?'

'That I don't, Cassidy. Your mam never said. I'm sorry.'

Cassidy would just have to phone the house. Her mother in England! She couldn't believe it. And poor grandfather! Was it because of her? It must be. What if he died? He couldn't. If he did she would have his death on her conscience for the rest of her life.

Mrs Mulligan was chattering on, but Cassidy wasn't listening, and as soon as she decently could, she said goodbye. As Bryan was upstairs she wasted no time in dialling her grandfather's number. She would explain to Bryan later.

The phone seemed to ring interminably. What if it was Leslie who answered? If the old man was ill, Leslie would be bound to be there. How was her mother getting on with him, she wondered.

She heard Mrs Dawson's voice. 'Hello. Berry House.'

'It's Cassidy,' she said simply.

'Oh, Cassidy, oh, thank goodness, love. Where on earth are you?'

Cassidy explained as briefly, as lucidly as possible.

Mrs Dawson went on. 'I don't blame you for running away, lass, I don't blame you for one minute, but do come back. He's badly and he's asking for you. Your mother's here, she's a grand woman. Shall I get her?'

'Yes, please,' Cassidy said.

Foolishly, as soon as she heard her mother's voice, she started to cry.

128

'Now, now, Cassidy.' Her mother's voice comforted her down the phone. 'Don't take on so. He's not dying. He has some paralysis and he did lose his speech but it's coming back. Oh, Cassidy, you're a wicked, wicked girl, going off like that. Are you with that Bryan?'

'Yes, I am. And "that Bryan" is the man I love, Mam, and I'm going to marry him. He's your nephew, you know.'

'So I've been told.'

'By Grandfather?'

'No, by Leslie. He's painted a rather lurid picture of you and your cousin, Cassidy. Running off together, indeed! Did I bring you up to do that?'

Cassidy sighed. 'Mam, you've only heard Leslie's side of the story. Do you like him? Tell me honestly, do you like him?'

There was a pause.

'No, I didn't think so,' Cassidy said.

'That's by the way,' Mary said. 'Are you coming home now? Dad wants to see you. All the time he's asking "Where's Cassidy?"'

'Yes, I'll come. Bryan doesn't know about Grandfather yet. I've only just come off the phone to Mrs Mulligan.'

'Is he a good man, Cassidy?' Mary sounded anxious.

'Oh, yes. I love him so much.'

'Esther's son. I can't believe it. And pretending he was somebody else.'

'I'll explain everything, Mam,' Cassidy
129

promised, but knew she wouldn't. Not everything.

When she had said goodbye to her mother, she went to find Bryan. How would he take this latest development? To Cassidy it seemed like an omen, a sign that they were meant to return to Yorkshire. Her grandfather kept asking for her. He was ill, he was vulnerable, he had already been reconciled with his daughter. It may be cruel, even heartless, but Cassidy believed there would never be a better time to go to him, to stand before him with Bryan at her side. To ask his forgiveness and to offer him their love.

The thing was, would Bryan see it that way?

CHAPTER TEN

Bryan came along willingly enough, but Cassidy knew it was only for her sake and that he wasn't looking forward to what he must believe would be an uncomfortable reception at the least. Just before they left he said, 'Things are moving too fast for me, Cassidy. I feel as though I'm being swept downstream, by a strong current I can't swim against. I don't like the feeling. I'm the sort of person who takes his time. I like to mull things over. I don't feel to be in control of my life any more.'

Cassidy kissed him warmly, wanting to

comfort him. 'What about you and me?' she said. 'You've hardly taken your time to decide you love me and want to marry me, have you?'

'No,' Bryan admitted, smiling, 'and just remember it's because I love you that I'm coming with you now to face that dreadful old man.'

'Now, now,' Cassidy chided. 'We know he isn't so dreadful.'

'Do we? Do we really? I haven't forgotten finding a very upset young woman in a churchyard not many days ago.'

Cassidy hadn't forgotten that incident either, but she did not want to be reminded of it.

'Let's go,' she said. 'Let's hit the road.'

Bryan's mood seemed to brighten as he put his arm around her shoulders and they walked outside, waving goodbye to Auntie Annie.

They arrived in Berrybridge some five hours later, having made one stop for refreshments as on their journey to Norfolk only days before. It was early evening, pleasantly cool after a rather sultry day. The village centre was quiet, with a sort of watchful, breath-holding air to it. Bryan parked the bike outside the house and they removed their crash helmets. Cassidy did not know whether to use the door-knocker or go straight in. She decided on the latter and Bryan followed silent and obedient behind her.

The first person they saw was Mrs Dawson who was just coming downstairs. She cried out and advanced on them, holding out her arms.

'Cassidy, oh, Cassidy, love!' she said.

They embraced. Then Cassidy said, 'This is Bryan. I suppose you've heard all about him by now.'

Mrs Dawson beamed, shaking Bryan's hand vigorously. 'Yes, I have and let me say you're very welcome, lad. I've seen you about, of course. You and your dog.'

'Oh, dear,' Cassidy began hesitantly, 'maybe we should have gone to see Amber first, to make sure she's all right.'

'No rush,' Bryan told her.

'How is Grandad?' Cassidy asked.

'Well, he's on the mend. But it'll be a slow job.'

'Was it my fault, Mrs Dawson?'

'Was what your fault? Oh, Lord, have mercy on us, course it wasn't. He's an old man. These things happen.'

'But he was upset, wasn't he, when I'd gone?' Cassidy persisted.

'Yes, he was and he ranted and raved, I must admit. We were all worried and upset, love.'

'Oh, I'm sorry.' Cassidy threw her arms around Mrs Dawson again and the housekeeper hugged her briefly before releasing her.

Her face had a cheerful expression.

'Now, nothing matters except you're both here. Safe and sound. Your mother's upstairs with him now.'

132

'Is Leslie here?' Cassidy ventured to ask, dreading the answer.

'No, thank goodness. He's driving me crazy, but he won't be here till tea time he said.' Her voice dropped to a conspiratorial whisper. 'I should go straight upstairs if I were you, love and happen it might be better if your young man waits down here to begin with.'

'Good idea,' Bryan said.

Cassidy glanced from one to the other of them. 'You're his grandchild, just as I am,' she reminded him, looking him straight in the eye.

Mrs Dawson broke in gently, 'All the same, Cassidy, just take it easy. I think that's for the best.'

Cassidy gave in. She had wanted them both to face Matthew together, but was well aware that Bryan was in no hurry to make that move. Because he had Mrs Dawson's approval, he was quite happy to go into the sitting-room whilst the housekeeper hurried away to put the kettle on.

Cassidy went upstairs alone. She could hear her mother's voice as soon as she drew near the old man's bedroom. She knocked gently on the door. Her mother opened it, her face flooding with relief and happiness when she saw Cassidy standing there.

'Cassidy!' They were in each other's arms.

'Bryan's downstairs,' Cassidy said. 'Mrs Dawson thought I should see Grandad alone first.'

133

'Yes, I think so, too,' Mary nodded in agreement. 'He's sitting up and is quite perky because we told him you were coming.'

'Is he cross with me, Mam?'

Mary smiled. 'He'll pretend to be, that's all.'

Cassidy squeezed her mother's hand. 'I'm glad you've made it up with him,' she said.

'So am I. And do you know, it wasn't so bad; in fact it was easy for both of us. So good's come out of bad, hasn't it?'

Remembering Bryan, Cassidy could only hope and pray her mother was right.

Mary said, 'I'd like to meet Bryan, shall I go down?'

'If you want to.'

A voice came from the bedroom, 'What are you blathering about, Mary? Has Cassidy come? Where is she?' The voice was quite strong and sturdy and some of Cassidy's apprehension about facing her grandfather vanished.

Mary pushed the door open. 'Go in, Cass. Don't be scared.' Her smile was encouraging and as her mother started for the head of the stairs, Cassidy walked into her grandfather's room, seeing the room for the very first time.

It was not much bigger than her own, but was much more severely decorated and furnished, with a huge mahogany bed and a matching wardrobe that took up most of one wall. The curtains were made of dark, heavy fabric and there was no carpet on the floor, only rugs on brown patterned vinyl. It was like stepping into the past. There was even a jug and bowl, blue and white patterned, on an old-fashioned, marble-topped washstand. Did he use it, Cassidy wondered.

Matthew Hawthorn was sitting up in bed, spruce and neat in a maroon, woollen dressing-gown over pyjamas. Apart from being pale where normally he was florid-faced, he didn't look any different to Cassidy. Until he beckoned her forward, using his right arm and she saw that his left hand lay limp against the eiderdown, the gnarled, old fingers curled as though they were hiding some secret object from view. Cassidy felt tears of pity for him and guilt for herself welling into her eyes.

She moved towards the bed. His eyes were red-rimmed and watering. On closer scrutiny she realised he was different. He looked much older, more tired. He leaned his head back against the heap of white pillows.

'So you're back,' he said shortly.

'Yes, Grandad,' Cassidy said meekly.

'What the devil do you mean by running off like that? Causing us no end of worry and trouble.'

'I'm sorry.' She forced herself to keep looking at him. 'Why did you send for Mam?'

He gave a short, harsh laugh. 'I didn't. It was that fool of a housekeeper who did that. Thought I was at death's door, I expect. Apparently, she found a telephone number in

135

your room.'

'So you're sorry Mam came, are you?'

'I didn't say that!' He shot the answer back at her. Then suddenly the anger seemed to drain out of him. He patted the bed. 'Oh, sit down, lass. I don't want to quarrel with you. You've been with that young chap, I understand?'

Cassidy nodded. 'With Bryan, your grandson, yes,' she admitted. 'We're going to get married.'

Cassidy braced herself for a fresh outburst, but none came. When Matthew spoke he even sounded amused.

'Oh, I see. Got it all planned, have you? What about Leslie?'

'What about him?' Their eyes met again, hers clear and young; his blurred and old. Then suddenly he burst out laughing.

'No-one's going to put you in your place, I can see that,' he chortled, wiping his eyes. With another swift change of mood he next spoke seriously. 'I suppose I'd better meet the chap. Esther's lad, eh? Will he stick a knife in me chest do you reckon?'

Cassidy smiled. 'I don't think so, Grandad,' she said.

He put his hand over hers, patting it gently. His fingers were cold.

'I know he must think the worst of me. You as well, I expect, and I know I haven't done much to make you like me. Shoving young

136

Leslie down your throat, but you do understand why, don't you, Cassidy? Now it doesn't seem so important any more. When I found you'd left, I was like a man bereft. Not again, I thought. I lost my lad, did you know—ay, course you must do, my son, James, when he was just twenty. Then there was my Mary, your mam, Cassidy. Took up with that worthless Paddy. I lost her, too. Esther gets herself into the family way and ... well, you know, as well as I do, that I threw her out. I'm not excusing myself, lass, I just want to tell it to you straight. Any road, I tried to get her back. I wrote her umpteen letters, but she never replied.' He paused. Cassidy said nothing, thinking of the pile of unopened letters she and Bryan had read. Thinking of the tin box and the secret it had revealed.

'But you've got Mam back, now, Grandad. And you've got me. And Bryan.'

He nodded his head slowly. 'Ay, you're right. And there's young Leslie. Now I know you don't think very highly of him, but he's a good lad; he's been good to me. Oh, I know he can be a pain in the neck, but he's my flesh and blood, you know, as well as you and Esther's boy.'

Cassidy bit her lip. Would she always feel a niggle of guilt at remarks like that?

'But, Cassidy, I want to tell you something else, now. Something I've told nobody before. When you've heard it, perhaps you'll be able to forgive and understand a stupid, old man who was once a young man, ay, and fit as a butcher's dog in them days, lass, young and very much in love. I bet that's floored you.'

Cassidy merely smiled. Matthew waved his hand towards the wardrobe. 'Fetch us that photo album,' he said, 'the one on the top of the pile.'

Cassidy did so and realised at once it was the album she herself had looked at and she knew when Matthew held it down with his weak arm and leafed through it with his good hand which picture he was looking for. The one of Elizabeth and the two older children, James and Esther. He sat and stared at it and then he began to talk and Cassidy listened to the account of the young Matthew Hawthorn's first meeting with the Irish girl, Elizabeth Cassidy.

He was on a business trip to Ireland with his father. He was twenty-seven and still a bachelor; a handsome, well-off, young fellow, who could have had his pick of girls; indeed his father was beginning to lose patience with what he called his son's shilly-shallying and larking around. Matthew saw Elizabeth as she helped wipe tables and clear away glasses in her father's pub. She was sixteen at the time and Matthew was completely smitten by the blue-eyed, raven-haired, Irish colleen.

From the moment he first set eyes on her, Matthew Hawthorn knew he had met the girl

138

he wanted to make his wife. He would not budge an inch from his resolve. His father tried all in his power to make him do so, but when Elizabeth Cassidy returned Matthew's feelings it was a lost cause.

Elizabeth had her parents' approval and backing, too. They were poor and had seven other children, all younger than Elizabeth. It pleased them to think of their beautiful daughter becoming a lady and marrying into wealth.

Matthew and Elizabeth were married that same summer, in a big, splendid Catholic wedding. Afterwards the newlyweds came back to Berrybridge and their life as husband and wife began.

Matthew closed the album but still held on to it. Cassidy waited breathlessly for him to continue his story.

At first they were blissfully happy. Maybe for a couple of years, at least until after their first child, James was born. Then in the year of the outbreak of World War Two, things began to change. Elizabeth began to grow restless for her homeland. It was not convenient for them to visit Ireland. The country was on the brink of war and sure enough Matthew was soon a member of the Armed Forces, serving as a commissioned officer in the Royal Artillery. When he was away from home, Elizabeth pined and moped, missing her husband, desperately homesick for Ireland.

By the time Matthew was invalided out of active service in late 1940 due to a leg injury, their marriage was very shaky. Esther was born but matters did not improve. Matthew began to lose patience with his wife as he saw her seeming to fade before his very eyes.

The war ended, Mary came along two years later. By then they were like two strangers. If only Matthew had not been so straight-backed, so unbending, there might have been hope. He could have compromised. He could have taken Elizabeth to Ireland, but he was what he was and his attitude towards Elizabeth only drove her further into herself. The more she pined and moped, the more disgusted and angry he became with her.

In 1948 Elizabeth Cassidy Hawthorn died. There was a flu epidemic at the time, but some said she died of a broken heart.

'So you see, lass,' Matthew concluded, tears running unheeded down his face, 'I lost her. The joy of my life. Elizabeth. I uprooted her, tearing up the delicate bloom in her youth and trying in vain to replant her in alien soil. And instead of sympathising with her, helping her, she irritated and annoyed me, because I couldn't stand her weakness and what I thought of as her disloyalty to me. I swore after Elizabeth died that none of my children would ever go through what she had gone through. I swore it, lass.'

Cassidy was beginning to understand. At

last! She imagined her mother announcing her love for Patrick O'Connor and her intention to marry him and settle in Ireland. Matthew must have seen it as a tremendous blow of fate. What if the same thing should happen to Mary, as had happened to Elizabeth? The despair, the pain, the gradual fading of life and will.

So in trying to prevent another tragedy, Matthew cut himself adrift from the daughter he loved so much, creating the very situation he was so desperate to avoid. By that time, James, the only boy, was dead. Matthew was left with Esther. When she, too, transgressed in her father's eyes, he must have been a very lonely, embittered man. At least with Esther he had done what he could to make amends, even if his efforts had been in vain.

Cassidy hugged the old man close to her. 'Oh, Grandad!' she cried. 'It's all right. You have me. You have Mam. And Leslie,' she added generously. 'We all love you. And now there's Bryan. Shall I bring him up? He's longing to meet you.'

He probably wasn't but she would prime him; make sure he smiled; make sure he was polite. Love would find a way. Bryan was not of Hawthorn blood but only she and he knew this.

One day, they would set out to trace his real parents, but that was for the future, the future they would now be facing together.

When Matthew held her away from him,

smiling through his tears, and said, 'Ay, go on, bring the lad in. And see you two get wed straight away. I want a great-grandson before I kick the bucket.' Cassidy knew that here and now, the deception did not matter in the slightest.

The LARGE PRINT HOME LIBRARY

If you have enjoyed this Large Print book and would like to build up your own collection of Large Print books and have them delivered direct to your door, please contact The Large Print Home Library.

The Large Print Home Library offers you a full service:

☆ **Created to support your local library**

☆ **Delivery direct to your door**

☆ **Easy-to-read type & attractively bound**

☆ **The very best authors**

☆ **Special low prices**

For further details either call Customer Services on 01225 443400 or write to us at:

The Large Print Home Library
FREEPOST (BA 1686/1)
Bath BA2 3SZ